VISITORS'
ARRIVAL

BOOK 3 OF THE LUNAR SERIES

JOSETH MOORE

authorHOUSE®

AuthorHouse™
1663 Liberty Drive
Bloomington, IN 47403
www.authorhouse.com
Phone: 1 (800) 839-8640

Published by AuthorHouse 07/29/2016

ISBN: 978-1-5246-2176-6 (sc)
ISBN: 978-1-5246-2175-9 (e)

Library of Congress Control Number: 2016912739

Print information available on the last page.

CONTENTS

This book is dedicated to my singer, my musician, my historian, & my Love, Deni. As well as to our kids, Darek, Felisha, & Gracie. And, finally, our departed Joe James Moore, & Dennis & Jackie Duntz...

CHAPTER 1

2217. SOL GOVERNANCE TERRITORY; PLANET-STATE PLUTO. TOMBAUGH MUNICIPAL...

The computer system ran its test for the fifth time, but there was no mistaking it: the ship was coming in from the Oort at 198,000 miles per second! The record for any human sub-light travel was still 172,000 mps. And even that was set back in the mid-22nd century when a group of humans were competing to see who could make it from Erth and fly out past State Pluto and back again. Humans, up to that point, had never achieved actual Light Speed since...so, clearly, the ship could not be human. Unless—

"May be there's a new competition going on that the Governance was not aware of," Sergeant Nesby ventured; not sounding like he believed it himself. The young man was craning his posture so he could get a better look at the image on his own terminal port.

"Why don't you do a search in the media and see if you can find any news on that, Sergeant," Director Morelli Tuun ordered. He was standing at his own terminal having trouble even believing the telemetry he was reading! "Whoever that is, they've got the fastest front velocity I've ever seen!"

Just to be sure, Tuun walked over to a nearby window and looked beyond the manicured grounds of State Pluto's domed city that served as the headquarters of the Sol Governance on Pluto. The object was still too far away to see with the naked eyes, but Director Tuun knew that he would be able to see it soon—given that the object was traveling faster than the speed of light!

"Sir," came Corporal Arund's voice from the other side of the Governance local facility, "satellites are picking up secondary object!"

Everyone in the large suite glanced at one another.

"Still could be a race, everyone," Director Tuun said as he walked back to his station and began doing a search on his terminal.

"Director Tuun, Sir," Sergeant Nesby's voice came back, "that's a negative on *any* private space competition anywhere in these parts of the solar system!"

"And we know the Governance does not obtain such technological ability to travel that fast, Director," added his lieutenant, Ron Ganum. Even though he was older than Director Tuun by several years, Ganum was Tuun's right-hand man in title *and* in his loyalty.

Tuun gave a long look at Ganum while the whole crew in the command center awaited the director's call. "This *cannot* be what I think it is!"

"First contact? It certainly looks that way, Director. Not counting the slugs on Callisto, of course."

The director rolled his eyes. "Those little bugs might as well be shower grout!"

Others nearby, including Ganum, shared a light chuckle. But then Director Tuun quickly got serious. He was already going through the official procedures in his head for the legendary *first contact* scenario that the Sol Governance had drilled into each and every officer within the solar system-wide political body...most of those military officials and political operatives had *never* thought there would be a time when The Governance would actually *use* those procedures! Without a word, Director Tuun gave a terse nod to Lieutenant Ganum, and the machine was set to motion!

"Ok, everyone," the lieutenant said as he scanned the entire command center; his voice at a booming level, "you heard the Director...let's get those auto-public messages and alarms going...Corporal, get our soldiers ready and their machines... Communications—alert headquarters! Something tells me we're going to need a little help out here!"

CHAPTER 2

SOL GOVERNANCE'S
HEADQUARTERS. PACIFICALIS
ISLAND; NORTHEAST OF THE
MARSHALL ISLANDS...

The Pacificalis Island landmass, itself, was human-made. It had been around since the mid-2100s. About that same time, when the majority of Erthen space-powers (both nations and private empires) got together to form the solar system-wide, governing organization known as the Sol Governance, they all wanted to build a headquarters that was *not* located in an existing nation-state. They often used as a reference the former United Nations, when it was based in the United States. Even though the global organization was meant to work objectively for the majority of Erth's nation-states, the fact that it was headquartered in the US meant that the former Superpower had disproportionate influences in many of the UN's votes...hence, The Governance's artificial island.

The unnaturally-round island was the size of a large island. Given that The Governance was a new form of political entity—part nation-state; part-corporation—the developmental planning was a hodgepodge of environmentally pleasing landscapes to industrial tracts of lands studded with belching buildings and horizon-stretching highways! Pacificalis also had suburban islands that were tethered to the mainland via high-tech bridges. Indeed, some of those suburbs were not even "islands" in the proper sense, but looming small cities on industrial stilts, much like the oil platforms back in the 20th and 21st centuries so long ago...

The Governance's main military complex was deep within Pacificalis' sprawling Humanity of approximately ten million. Admiral Reshma Shan was in charge of running Governance's military sector on Pacificalis. She was approaching senior status in society and was looking forward to retirement. But until those next few years came, Admiral Shan still had a lot on her plate. In addition to the bite-sized wars that seemed the norm for modern warfare on planet Erth, she was also the charge for helping citizens in natural disasters on all the planetary and lunar bodies of the Sol system. Today, the admiral would have to take on a lot more duties for humanity.

"Admiral...Admiral," the young cadet was calling out to Shan. He was trotting up to the admiral as she just left a meeting in one of the Governance's weekly briefings of high officers.

She turned from her chat with a couple of other officers and gave them a friendly wave goodbye. But that warm demeanor had melted away upon seeing the cadet.

"What's the problem, Grainger?"

He simply held up his communicator, which was displaying a message from one of the Governance's outer provinces. It was Director Tuun's base, and it was urgent! The projected info flashed text and images for references, and the admiral got exactly what the situation was.

Shan looked around to make sure no one else could hear them.

"So, no one's been able to contact them since," she whispered.

"Three days...Correct," Cadet Grainger simply stated. He was actually shaking! Shan reasoned that he, perhaps, had someone special to him in the Pluto settlements.

"And what about Director Graffs and her people in all this...why didn't the Charon's Watch notice this?"

"That's the other problem, Admiral..." The cadet entered a command on his device and the holographic info switched to data on the town-sized base on Pluto's largest moon, Charon. "Watcher 7 went silent not much longer when Pluto did!"

Admiral Shan thought for a long moment within the bustling base. Grainger patiently waited for her next orders.

"Pretty bad when the watchman goes missing, huh?"

"Yes, Ma'am...you want me to contact Watcher 6 and have them send over a team, ma'am?"

"Which indicates that Watcher 6 either doesn't know what happened to their buddies on Watcher 7, or they're waiting for my call," she said with some irritation.

Grainger, slight in build; young, measured his response. "Frankly, Admiral, we were having difficulties reaching them, too!"

The towering Shan sharply twisted her head to face the cadet directly.

"It, it was some kind of interference, but Watcher 6 is all-go, Admiral."

"And do you think it's any coincidence that 6 is experiencing some *interference*, Grainger," she retorted as she, now, whipped out her own communicator and began to place lines of communications. "One by one, Cadet, we seem to be losing our stations in the Kuiper region..." Not wanting to cause panic among the officers in the immediate area, Admiral Shan furtively shared her contacts with Grainger and quietly reached one of the commanding officials of a secret status within Sol Governance's military...

CHAPTER 3

ABOARD *THE JUSTIFIER*, SOL GOVERNANCE'S SPECIAL ASSIGNMENT SOLAR CRAFT; ORBITING NEREID, MOON OF NEPTUNE...

Joden Modune was still in the process of writing up his list of projects for his crew on his terminal when he had gotten a call from headquarters. He was already running late—his Medium-sized special operations team was finished running tests and drills and were waiting for Joden's next orders. But the fact that he was being called from HQ, versus receiving a message informing him of an upcoming call, there was no doubt that it was something important!

"Jaimee, I've got a comm coming from Pacificalis," Joden informed his second-in-command. "I'm going to need you to get everyone geared up."

"Right, boss," she punched out over the line.

The chiming from communications was not even registering with Joden. His mind started to wander off into various scenarios what headquarters wanted this time around...

"Modune, Ma'am," he finally said to Admiral Reshma Shan. She wasn't even impatient with him about how long it took for Joden to answer.

"Joe, we've got some problems going on around the Pluto area and it looks like it's heading *your* way," she shot out. The admiral's eyes were periodically bouncing up and down and off to the side from various screens that were out of the line of sight on the broadcast, Joden noticed. "For some reason no one in the system can get in contact with Pluto, Watch 7, and, *now*, Watch 6..."

Joden froze in his chair. She was right: *The Justifier* was next in line! The admiral continued.

"We've already notified Watcher 5— no sense in telling the other stations until necessary. They have enough to worry about...Director Nadeem is sending over a squadron from 5 to join up with you all, Joe. By that time, based on the timing that we've lost communications with everyone so far, you and Director Nadeem should be in a position to carry out whatever tactics and strategies you need to do to confront whatever it is."

"Ma'am," Joden asked with a snap of his head toward his monitor.

"Honestly, Joe, we don't know." The admiral finally sat back; looking at Joden straight in the eyes—as it were—over her monitor, her head shaking for bewilderment. "Cadet Grainger was the last to talk with Director Furth before Watcher 6 went down...Grainger lost total contact with 6!"

All that the admiral could do at that time was shrug. Joden silently nodded in confirmation.

"Good luck, Joe," Admiral Shan said with seemingly sincerity. "Keep me updated...I'll let you know if there are any developments."

"Understood, Ma'am."

The admiral cut the line; leaving a blank space where the projected holographic image once levitated. Joden, his dark-set eyes unblinking, stared at that spot for several more seconds. The thirty-something captain of the *"undeclared class"* solar ship had a passing thought.

"Sentient, give me a map of the solar region, depicting Uranus and all the way to the Oort cloud...also, input symbols for all Watcher bases, space stations, and ships in the area in real time, please."

In the middle of Captain Modune's cabin appeared a large, holographic "textured map." The region of space that the captain requested was shown in slightly stylized details with touch-capabilities for the user to easily move any images depicted. The map also showed *The Justifier's* location within the representation. Captain Modune's crew was orbiting just outside of Nereid; between it and Neptune—which filled most of the vista of the ship's windows and monitors displaying the near-space in *Justifier's* neighborhood.

Modune maneuvered the room-sized map with the movement of his hands so that the map showed a close-up of Sol's region with Saturn, Uranus, Neptune, Pluto, the Kuiper belt, and the Oort cloud... all were iconofied, but realistic enough to get which planets and moons were at play. He, then, walked up to the portion of the hologram that displayed a large swath of the Oort and Kuiper sections—for it seemed whatever was coming its way to Neptune had originated from there. If not, then passed through, perhaps.

Modune thought on the various articles and media reports he'd read or watched about some of the scientific projects in both the Belt and the Cloud. He could not think of any current research project going on in those regions at that time. Nevertheless... He addressed his 'Sentient' once again.

"Sentient, search for any scientific research, for any military operations, or any natural, known occurrences going on in this region of space—" Captain Modune drew a large, irregular box that framed most of the space depicting the region.

The Justifier's computer system took a little longer than usual before it super-imposed images of boxes, floating telemetry, and its female voice responded.

"There are currently no activities of scientific research, or military operations, nor any natural occurrences transpiring at this time that are outside the usual cycles and schedules."

Joseth Moore

"Then what's that blip you have there," Modune refuted, as he walked up to a portion of the holographic map. "Here—around the 10 to the fourth power AU?" Modune touched the irregular-shaped beacon, but no information emitted from the floating shape.

"That, Captain, is one of the Governance's distance-markers," the computer responded; somewhat condescendingly.

"Damn it, Sentient, I've flown the Sol for years. I *know* what and where our distance-markers are! I don't remember *that* one in particular."

"Shall I notify Watcher 5's squadron captains of this apparent anomaly, Captain Modune?"

"Please...while you're at it, tell the crew to get situated and then fly us out to those coordinates."

"Yes, Captain. And what of the crews of Pluto State and station Watchers 7 and 6?"

Modune paused in his tracks; getting his travel gear ready. "That squadron from Watcher 5 should catch up with us by the time we get to Pluto, right?"

"Correct, Captain. But we will by-pass station Watcher 6 and Pluto's crew on the course you've given...with all the event anomalies going on in the Pluto-area recently, should we not stop to check on them?"

By this time, Captain Modune had finished donning his activity jumpsuit. "I figured the ships from Watcher 5's squadron should fly over to Watcher 6 and check on Pluto. They have enough crew to divide up the task between the base on Pluto and the Watch station on Charon...How does that compute? Is my logic sound, Sentient?"

"Indeed. But, may I ask, Captain, why you feel *The Justifier* should take on the task of seeking out this apparent anomaly at distance-marker 10 to the fourth power?"

Now, Modune was holding his personal space-helmet and standing next to the door to his suite. "First of all, Sentient, *Justifier's* crew is a nondeclared operation—since that anomaly is unknown as well as the status of all the stations in the Pluto-area, it would be better for *our* team to take it on instead of Watcher 5's squadron...should the situation out there turn out to be dire, *Justifier's* crew should quietly inform Headquarters.

"Secondly, I don't think that's a distance-marker. I think it's a Trojan horse!"

CHAPTER 4

It had been nearly a day later since Captain Modune's crew was activated by Admiral Shan for the Pluto-situation. *The Justifier's* young crew of twenty had already passed planetary Station Watcher 6 and was headed out for Pluto and its moon, Charon, with Squadron B close behind. Captain Liz'Beth's team from that squadron was assigned to Charon's Watch planetary gate while Captain Modune's special ops crew had the biggest assignment in the planetary station located on Pluto itself. Modune had gotten word from Captain Lance Ward of Squadron A that he and his crew had finally reached Watcher 6 station...

"Gone," Captain Modune heard himself say a bit louder than he meant to during his communique with Captain Ward. Modune was in the main cabin area of *The Justifier*, so all of his crew could hear the conversation. "Captain, when you say, 'gone'—"

"As in it looks like the freakin' Rapture just happened," the middle-ager said with absolutely no irony! He was peering at Captain Modune over his spectacles on the connection while his crew, in the background, could be seen quickly working on their terminals and scurrying about! "Tables and chairs tipped over; dishes on the floors; equipment strewn about..."

Modune thought for a moment as he glanced about his own cabin, seeing what his own, tight-knit crew thought so far. He was met with shrugs, stares, and arched brows.

"So," Modune ventured on; trying to understand a bit more, "no signs of blood or weapons used?"

"Right...now, Joe, don't get me wrong. It looks as if the whole damn station left in a hurry—like they were trying to catch a shuttle or something. But I wouldn't say it looks like there was a struggle here, as such."

Now Captain Modune's team really looked upon him with incredulity!

"Speaking of shuttle," Modune went on, "what about 6's shuttles and androids?"

"All here," Captain Ward said matter of factly. "We just checked their task records and there's not a single entry for any of the shuttles, androids—or emergency pods, for that matter—that were engaged. Hell, even the station's kitchens are in decent shape!"

"Food, Captain," Jaimee Box, Modune's second-in-command, asked with a whisper; out of range of Captain Ward's sight. "Was anything left on?" Others in *Justifier's* cabin were nodding in consent.

"Was anything left boiling or in one of the cooking machines, Lance," Modune tried.

Captain Ward was already shaking his head. "Nope...not so much as a kettle of tea was on! Even their Sentients greeted us upon our arrival as if nothing were wrong! Huh...I think whatever got our people also got to their Sentients. We went around and around with them trying to see if they saw anything or recorded whatever happened."

"And...?"

"Nothing! It's like someone wiped the crew's entire computer system and re-started them!"

Commander Box made a questioning face to the response. Others in the cabin looked away at some corner; trying to make sense of the whole ordeal.

"Well, that pretty much leaves you with checking their on-board recorders then, Lance," Joden said after gauging his crew in the command center.

Captain Ward had leaned back in his chair with a knowing sigh. "And *that*, my friend, is when things get even more interesting...they all stopped!"

"Stopped?" Now Modune's crew had gone beyond curious looks to that of concern. Captain Modune went on. "Every recorder on the station?"

"Well, that's what my team has encountered so far, Joe," Captain Ward said as he looked off to the side; verifying with one of his officers. "We're still in the process of checking and re-checking those we've already gone through—we get a look at Station 6's crew from about two days ago. And..." Ward shrugged at that point; his head shaking with bewilderment. "*Every* damn recorder stopped and goes blank at the exact same time! Not just the holographs; even our 2D backups, Joe!"

"Lance, what do they show the crew doing just before the records blank out?"

"Well, the ones from Watcher 7's command cabin show Director Graffs' crew positioning themselves at their stations...I'm not sure I'd say they seemed like they were in distress or anything—"

"But purposeful," Captain Modune interjected with the nod of his head.

"Yeah...as for the other bases, Joe," Captain Ward said over the communique with a shrug, "it's like they didn't even see anything coming... What are you thinking, Captain?"

"Trojan horse," Captain Modune said as he brought up his search-history from his personal quarters. He shared the entire search-event with Captain Ward through their communique. "Right after Admiral Shan assigned me to this, I did a little research of the Pluto area...I can't be exactly sure, Lance, but I have a suspicion about one of the Governance's stationary markers out there. I couldn't bring up any info on it—"

"Distance-marker 10," Ward said with a smirk as he leaned back in his command seat.

Joden froze for surprise. "So, you've noticed, too?"

"Mmm...I figured it was just another piece of real estate that we didn't have logged into our system. Shows that you're far more observant than I am, Captain!"

"I've got an idea for testing my hypothesis..." Everyone in Captain Modune's command suite shot a look in his direction. "I'll contact you whatever the results are."

Ward nodded and disconnected their communique.

CHAPTER 5

Admiral Reshma Shan's basic idea for the Pluto-area mystery was to have the planetary space station Watcher 5 send over one squadron with Captain Modune's team and have the squadron divide up in two—that way there was a team to investigate the situations in station Watcher number 6; the other half of the squadron go to Watcher number 7, which was on Pluto's moon of Charon; and leave the main job of the station *on* Pluto for Modune and his crew.

Modune and his crew were one of those special operations assets that military space powers relied on when they needed a vanguard to check out a situation and to triage whether or not it was worth said-space powers to expend a more serious presence in the outer region of the Sol system. Aside from the government of the Sol Governance, even private space powers had adopted such philosophies...and the situation that *The Justifier* crew had found themselves in, definitely needed some serious triaging!

Captain Modune had the crew land *Justifier* down in Pluto's craggy mountainous region nicknamed 'the Snakeskins.' Over the years of developing the planetoid of Pluto, the Sol Governance had learned that the series of mountains were a good hiding place, given that the region's surface would often breakup various signals! And if Captain Modune was right about the house-sized, distance marker in the Kuiper belt region being some kind of Trojan deception, then *Justifier's* crew would fight fire with fire...he left that task to his second-hand; Commander Jaimee Box.

In the meantime, the Captain had to set off with a smaller party to go to the Governance's Pluto base where Director Morelli Tuun and the entire Tombaugh Municipal had not been heard from for several days! Deep down inside, Captain Modune doubted that Admiral Shan would have approved of him splitting up an already small special ops team and sending one fraction to the small city of Tombaugh and the rest hiding in their ship within the Snakeskin mountains—waiting for Commander Box to spring whatever trap awaited them in the Kuiper belt... but Joden could not see any other way of tackling the events in the Pluto region.

Captain Modune's auxiliary team's tiny speeder craft, chevroned in shape and flat, sped into the small city-base of Tombaugh; named after a then-American astronomer whom discovered Pluto 287 years previously. To call the municipal a "city" was actually artistic. Tombaugh was really just a large base comprising of clusters of domes and roadways...the biggest structure in the town was Tombaugh's main, towering dish communications system the size of one of Erth's high-rise buildings. But of the approximate population of 5,000, not a single person was in sight; walking around in their space suite, driving along the utilitarian road system, or otherwise! Captain Modune reminded the 5 others in the speeder what Captain Ward had said earlier about the recordings of the three bases. And how the holographic records simply stopped and station 6 was simply abandoned.

"This is just weird," Corporal Eric Esstint commented as Captain Modune piloted the speeder to a landing platform within Tombaugh.

"Do you think it's possible they willingly left," Sergeant Beatrice Pfilster speculated as she and the others gathered their gear. The team was already suited up in their space suits and were filing out of the ship.

They were communicating via their suits' comm system. "May be some kind of political dispute? I've seen in the media how there are more independence movements within a lot of these outposts beyond Mars and the Asteropia belt!"

"But how would that fit with the holo-recordings *and* the 2-D backups *all* stopping at the same time," Lieutenant Nolla Massett, the second-in-command of the auxiliary team, asked with incredulousness.

"If it were some organized effort, I could see that," Sergeant Chris Sheets added, as the whole team stood and thought things through; yet by the parked speeder. Sheets' point had resonated with the rest of the team as they all nodded.

"Alright," Captain Modune finally said, after waiting to see if anyone else in the team had any other input, "since Tombaugh is such a small locale we'll go ahead and split up in 2 groups... Nolla, why don't you take Sheets and

Esstint. Pfilster; Utan, that leaves the three of us..."

The 2 groups headed in different directions within the base.

"Everyone's suit charged up in case we need to use our jets," the captain said over the com as the team went on with their mission.

"*Charged, Sir,*" came the unison response over the com. Joden merely nodded to himself...

A few hours had passed by and the auxiliary team found nothing of significance, outside of more of the same abandoned space-ghost town they had already seen: like what Captain Lance Ward's crew had found in space station Watcher 6, the base on Pluto had *no* signs of struggle nor force; civilian items simply left in place, not *dropped* or anything; and yet no people! Even more, all of the known Governance-issued vehicles were parked in their respective docks or platforms. Modune's team were able to tell this given the solar system-wide government had standard procedures for stowage of ships and other crafts when they were not in use.

It did not take long for the auxiliary team's 2 groups to search the entire outpost, given its size. All 6 were back in the mid-section of the town, congregated by the towering dish communications structure. Then Captain Modune's comm chirped. It was Commander Box calling from *The Justifier*. The rest of Modune's team glanced about as he took the call.

"Jaimee," the captain said; a bit anxious, "have you started that mission with the distance-marker yet?"

"Yes, Sir...about an hour ago, actually." Modune and Box were visually connected. He was using his comm that was embedded in his space suit on his left forearm. "I'm patching you all to the live-feed. It'll just be a few more minutes before the decoy reaches the proper-space of the distance-marker...if that's what it is!"

"Great," he said as he looked around at his small team; indicating that they needed to link onto their own visual com to watch as well. "We got nothing down here, Jaimee...heard from Ward or Liz'Beth?"

"I heard from them, Captain. But it was the same as you: still no signs of any of the personnel on either Watcher 6 nor Charon!"

There was nothing else for them to do at that point but wait for the secondary mission to proceed. Captain Modune glanced at his team to gauge *their* unspoken opinions...mostly there were shrugs. Corporal Thomas Utan was the only one with a question.

"Decoy, Sir?"

"Yeah, the Commander and I thought we'd test the waters and see if that marker is a trap—"

"This Trojan horse you spoke of?"

"Only, *we're* sending something out to check on the 'Horse' before *us*," Sergeant Pfilster remarked; nodding her head with approval of the tactic.

"Yep," Modune said. "We had an exploratory pod to spare, so Box had Cadet Mohadeen retrofit it with fake life readings...Alright, we're going to wait here while we monitor your mission, *Justifier*; just in case there's some kind of action that may implicate Pluto's base..." Now Modune shook his head; still bewildered of the situation.

Commander Box was watching *The Justifier's* main screen at the head of the command suite's room as she spoke. "The decoy should be entering...*now*."

On everyone's monitor, the live feed from the decoy-pod displayed the floating, rectangular marker— having 6 sides; which typically were glorified, 5-storied electronic boxes that displayed information about the local space-region should any space craft had broken down and lost main, electronic functions. In a word, distance-markers were basically floating information traffic signs for space-traffic, *and* served as emergency stations. They were prevalent in the Sol system's inner-core region with all of Humanity's permanent space-traffic. *And* they were big enough to house a small ship of people with nefarious intentions...definitely *not* big enough to conceal a battle ship, but, again, in the Greek legend of the Trojan horse, all it took was a few men to open the gates...

CHAPTER 6

SOL GOVERNANCE'S HEADQUARTERS. PACIFICALIS ISLAND...

"...Admiral," David Thompson, one of the other cadets at the Sol Governance's headquarters, called out to her as she was about to board her personal craft to attend a global meeting in continental Europe. She had just stepped on the platform to board the planetary craft when Thompson had stopped her. She had a very indignant look on her face when she turned to see who it was. "Ma'am... you're definitely going to want to see this! It's about *The Justif—*"

"Say no more, Cadet," she stopped him. *The Justifier* crew was *never* to be mentioned out in public! Admiral Shan called over the pilot of the ship, and with a snapping nod of understanding, the pilot ran back into the craft and disengaged the engine.

Admiral Shan was following Cadet Thompson back to her personal quarters where it was secured for them to talk. After her door sealed shut, she started to curse the young one for nearly exposing the non-declared mission before he beat her to the punch.

"They're gone, Ma'am!"

She stood in shock, and perhaps not sure she understood the cadet. "You mean *Justifier's* crew?"

"Yes, Ma'am. Just like the bases out in Pluto's region...Cadet Grainger is busy trying to contact them one more time in the secured room after we got word from space station Watcher 5. I thought you might want to know before going on your meeting, Ma'am."

The admiral's mood went straight from boiling hot to down-right alarmed! How does an administrator deal with the fact that their special ops team sent to survey and secure a situation ends up *missing* just like those they were meant to help? There was no getting around it...whoever, or *whatever*, was out there in the outer regions of the Sol system was very close to checkmating planet Erth at this rate!

"Ma'am...?"

"Yes, Cadet...I, I think it's time we convey an emergency meeting of the Governance at once! We don't have time for a physical sit-down right now...have Grainger help you set up the necessary contacts."

"Yes, Ma'am," Thompson snapped, and he raced out of her secured quarters.

CHAPTER 7

Even though Admiral Shan was already in Sol Governance's headquarters it was no guarantee that the hundreds of other solar system-wide officials would be there to conveniently meet with her! Indeed, about half of the several hundreds of representatives of the Governance's Erthen, lunar, and space station sovereigns were in their home-regions, tending to other businesses in other parts of the Sol system, or just plain old on vacation and it was pretty much impossible to find them! It made no matter. One of the cornerstone ordinances of the Governance was when there was an existential emergency, quorum-rules were superseded *by* that emergency! Whether members physically attended meetings or whether they met via virtual quorums, the existential emergency took precedence.

There were a few times in its 91 years of existence that the Sol Governance had to convene due to existential threats: one time was when an asteroid clipped one of the moons of Jupiter and caused a "shower" of meteors to pulverize nearby space stations and lunar settlements that, in total, represented approximately 10 million solar system citizens! Another time was entirely human-made... when a nationalistic resurgence of an ancient lunar culture known as Tellmondo had sprung up throughout near-Erth space and those of ethnic Tellmondonian lineage had gone on some bombing sprees; killing tens of thousands of *non*-Tells. Indeed, some in the solar system had considered the military battles against the revived

Tellmondonian movement as the Sol system's *first* "Solar War!"

Since such upheavals, the Sol system had been relatively quiet. Until now...

"...Admiral Shan, I consider this a betrayal," privateer real estate owner, Vornan Huntworth, scolded over the virtual link for the Governance emergency meeting. Admiral Shan had simply conducted the meeting from her personal quarters since it was of high-quality security and the lack of time for all of them to travel. The suite was hers, personally, and she paid for the higher cost for being in "the nice neighborhood" within the many halls of Governance headquarters. The meeting had been going on for approximately thirty minutes. "Everyone knows I own several space stations out by station Watcher 5...my people that work those space stations *and* the stations themselves are next in line of whatever this is that's coming our way! You should have informed me the second you knew about this situation!"

Shan knew it was not logical, but she wanted to strike the tiny holographic image of the middle-aged man for being so narrow-minded at such a time. "Mr. Huntworth, I suggest that you focus on helping the Council find out what, exactly, it is that we're even dealing with! Look, I told you I sent out a special operations team to get a handle on the events before we reacted—"

"And how's that going for ya," the wealthy real estate owner said sarcastically.

There was a thud in the virtual meeting from the Council's chair, Xi Zehan; one of the Governance's youngest chair, being in her 30s. "Members, please, we do not have time for this bickering..." Chair Xi's holo-image turned to look upon Admiral Shan—from Shan's point of view. "Admiral, I have to admit, Member Huntworth has a valid point. Had the

Council been aware of these events, we would have been days in advanced on working with you on this problem... is there anything else you can tell us about the *Justifier* mission that might help us speed this along?"

The admiral was already shaking her head. "No more than what I've already told the Council...like I said, the last transmission we got from *Justifier's* crew was of them sending some kind of probe to an uncharted distance-marker that they, I guess, had some kind of suspicion about."

The hundreds of holograms of the representatives, arranged in tight-rectangles in a grid-fashion with each respective Member in front of Shan as she sat at her desk, was all evenly projected as a wall of tiny faces with telemetry floating about. Each user of the virtual interfacer had the option of enlarging, highlighting, and other editing features of these meetings. The chair, whomever it was at any time, controlled who got to speak and they were known to simply cut any Member's transmitted image if that Member went on too long, or became too hostile!

"A distance-marker," Alexandr Tulman, the president of Israel and another younger Member, asked incredulously.

"I know, Member Tulman," Admiral Shan acknowledged. "My people and I didn't understand why they were so fixated on a space-marker when all these events were going on. But Captain Modune's team kept referring to the Trojan horse legend..." She shrugged as others in the meeting voiced concerns, questions, and criticisms.

Again, that ancient sound of a block of wood being struck by a wooden gavel. Chair Xi went on. "I think we should send special ops to *every* marker in the solar system!"

Now, there was an uncomfortable silence until Member Veronica Peters, the CEO of Peters' Bank—Sol, spoke up. "*Every distance-marker,* Chair Xi? In the whole of the Governance? Ma'am, do you know how many *thousands* of space-markers there are?"

Admiral Shan began rubbing her face out of frustration from the arguing in the meeting! She said nothing.

"I do," Chair Xi responded. "And I know we have enough personnel to investigate each and every one of those markers! If it's true what Admiral Shan said about *Justifier's* crew believing a distance-marker as being some kind of decoy, then, what about the thousands of *other* markers in the Sol system? Or, at least, some *pretending* to be the Governance's markers!"

By then, the virtual meeting erupted with jeers from most of the Members in the Council. And, again, the gavel was rapping against its block.

"Based on the timing of events, fellow Members," Chair Xi *informed* the Council, "I move that I emplace emergency codifications of the Sol Governance's Constitution and assume emergency powers...Guards," she exclaimed as she summoned them, whom were out of visual range, "assemble my staff at my office—drag them there if you must. We are now officially under Existential Emergency Codification...you all must go through your constitutional procedures appropriately..." At that point, Chair Xi returned her gaze to her own holographic wall of representatives. "My fellow Members, we all know the procedures on *our* end. Some of you are new to your positions. I suggest that you consult your top staff *and* refer to your manuals."

No one else in the virtual assembly said a word. Indeed, many of the Council's Members were solemn or nearly at tears! Chair Xi Zehan looked directly at Admiral Reshma Shan; no emotion that Shan could see.

"Admiral...despite your poor judgement in delaying to contact the Council, I commend you for bringing this to our attention." The admiral

Visitors' Arrival

silently nodded back a 'thank you.' Xi went on to say to the admiral, "You'll have to send reinforcements to space station Watcher 5, Admiral. Coordinate with Director Nadeem and see what they all need out there."

"Yes, Chair Xi."

Chair Xi once again looked upon the hundreds of thumbnail-holos silently looking directly at her. "Alright, Members...So, now, we need to redeploy some of our forces to monitor *any* false space-markers we may have in the whole solar system!"

CHAPTER 8

Hours had gone by since Admiral Reshma Shan convened the Sol Governance's emergency meeting, and there was still no sign of not only the *Justifier's* crew, but nothing from Director Dian Graffs' crew from lunar station Watcher 7, nor Director Heather Furth's people in Watcher 6, and the same went with the Planet-State Pluto base under Director Morelli Tuun...it had now been *days* since anyone from the Governance had heard from those soldiers! And at some point, whatever the phenomenon was, it was heading straight for Erth!

Admiral Shan needed time to brainstorm. She let her staff take over for her in the command center as she bunkered down in her command suite. She pulled up all her terminal capabilities to game out possibilities of various, unlikely-to-likely invasions within the solar system. Her personal Sentient swatted down most of the hypotheses—from cult-terrorist organizations connected to the Tellmondonians, to Sentient programs that had gone rogue and were scheming to obliterate the human race!

But there was one possible scenario that the admiral's Sentient kept going back to with every model she threw at it...

"...I'm sorry, Sentient, but humans have heard about the threat of alien invasions for hundreds of years now! The only other beings we know about outside of Erth are the Callistonian slugs!"

"I know," her Sentient responded; a bit pompous, "and you humans were so disappointed in them since they weren't your 20th century, little green men...that is, until you started harvesting the poor species for your super-speed space travels!"

"Ok, Sentient... one of the last things I need to hear right now is a lecture from a computer about how *its* masters are imperfect!"

"Ouch..."

Shan got up from her seat and began to pace. "So, you really don't see any of the political groups in the outer parts of the solar system even having the capability to build ships to go this fast?"

"No, Admiral. Not based on current media reports. Only wealthy citizens *within* Sol's core worlds currently have such abilities. And, as of now, based on governmental reports and cultural media, there are no indications any of those wealthy citizens have a hand in this. Besides the near-light speed abilities, who else of the human race would have the ability to disable *all* of the Governance's Sentients *without* having to stop, and *then* tinker with all those systems? To say nothing of the mass abductions at *each* space station!

"With each model that we game, as you put it, Admiral, the likelihood always comes down to some *alien* agency."

Admiral Shan went silent for a long while as she thought on every morsel of information she had gotten between the Governance's emergency meeting and the one she, currently, was in with her Sentient. She continued to pace; glancing at telemetry floating at various terminal sites...

"You know," she finally said, "it's a damn shame that we, humans, feel this way of the possibility of an alien encounter. Long ago, there was a time when we relished the idea of even *seeing* one with one of those old rovers humans used to send to other planets! But now..." She solemnly shook her head; finding a place to rest her hands on as she stopped her pacing.

The Sentient's chime-indicator rang. "Admiral, Doctor Franks is at your door, Ma'am."

She straightened up from her slouched position. "Thanks, Sentient... let her in, please."

The door to the admiral's quarters slid opened and the tall, slender woman—elderly—wasted no time as she plowed in. She wore a modern-day robe attire; a style that was heavily influenced by the old Tellmondonian ways. It was rumored by some at the Governance's headquarters that, perhaps, she was a Tell' descendent. She was one of many Governance's scientists that belonged to the semi-autonomous institution called the Physical Universities. Indeed, the Universities employed many Tellmondonians and other cultural movements and political-thoughts that often served more as a counter-balance to the military powers within the solar system-wide Governance body than they served as the

Governance's scientists! "Reshma, have you heard what they're doing?"

The admiral looked at her friend and colleague with confusion.

Dr. Franks tsked, rolled her eyes up toward the ceiling and spoke to the Sentient. "Sentient, please show the admiral the news of today from the Governance's Members!"

Immediately, a holographic sphere appeared in the center of Admiral Shan's quarters. It was a recorded news-feed from various sources throughout the solar system. It was news that happened since the admiral's meeting with the Governance's Members...

The media report showed recorded events of Sol Governance military soldiers from various branches of the solar government lining up in large hangars throughout the solar system. Most of the soldiers were already boarding massive battle spaceships, apparently all sparked by the alarming disappearances of space bases further out in the solar system! *But* it was this phenomenon that the admiral could not share with anyone outside the Governance's Members-institution.

"Is this the Members," Dr. Franks tersely put to her friend and colleague.

"Yes," Admiral Shan responded directly. She did not even try to do the usual elusive replies that government officials often do when addressing a difficult subject. "Look, Urla, I know how the Governance's scientists feel about first uses of military force, but it should tell you that it must be something so serious that the Members ordered a massing of troops without warning! Urla, things are so serious that I can't even risk telling *you* right now!"

The elderly woman flinched out of surprise. She looked upon the admiral with incredulous eyes. "Is this a First Contact scenario, Reshma?"

"Urla..." Admiral Shan gave her a warning look.

The scientist nodded; giving up her protest. "What can we, at the Universities, do to help, Admiral?"

"Just—please, keep an eye out for anything *highly* unusual..." The scientist made a confused looked with her face, but Admiral Shan kept her focus. "I really can't say much more, Urla. If any of the scientists, staff, or even the students see highly irregular things going on you've got to tell one of us from the Governance."

Dr. Franks was obviously caught off guard with such vague—yet, aggressively serious—remarks by her friend, that she almost felt that their friendship was being tested. Dr. Franks turned to leave the admiral's suite; feeling dejected.

"Don't fly near any distance-markers..."

Admiral Shan's whispered warning stopped Dr. Franks. She turned to face her long-time friend. Understanding what the admiral was trying to do, Franks silently nodded a 'thanks' to her, and left the admiral's suite.

CHAPTER 9

———————✦———————

Hours later, Admiral Reshma Shan's suite...

When she got out of bed to answer the call it was just after 2 in the morning. She still had her uniform on from the previous day!

Shan glanced at the interface to see who it was and to scan any newsflashes she might need to know about. She engaged the comm and it brought up Cadet Shawn Grainger's young face. "Report, Cadet..."

"Ma'am, Communications just got the best lead of what's happened to *Justifier's* crew!"

Well, that caused the admiral to shoot straight up from her bed! She listened on.

"It's footage from a private automaton that works for TQF Kuiper. It was working on a mining project for its company on Pluto...now, it was several miles away from Tombaugh municipal, where Captain Modune and some of his officers were located at the time, but the recording is good enough to give us a clue what happened!"

The admiral merely nodded; waiting for the cadet to patch the recording to her comm...

The footage was a bit shaky and slightly out of focus. Given that the autonomous mining-android was one of several robotic androids working at a quarry when it captured the footage, it was no surprise to Admiral Shan. Indeed, she had a thought, upon seeing some of the other auto-miners in the recording.

"Grainger, how far did this recording go?"

"As in, was it able to function when the recordings at the other sites all simultaneously stopped?"

By this time, Admiral Shan was walking over to her terminal. "Exactly."

"The recording goes on for several more minutes—really, a *lot* longer. We just extracted the footage relevant to our investigation."

At that point, the recording was still of nothing more than of a landscape on Pluto with the township of Tombaugh in the distance with all its lights and a few of the other auto-miners working.

"I *still* wonder why those automatons were not affected by the blackout, like what happened at our bases," she said out loud; more to herself than to the cadet.

Both had gone silent as they watched and listened to the recording...

The icy and rocky placid scene on Pluto with town-Tombaugh in the distance and the autonomous drones digging suddenly flashed brightly—as if a star had exploded! The flashing pulsated, but unevenly, and within seven seconds the landscape went right back to the mostly-dark setting it was before. Even the modular-town's lights were still on...

Via his comm, Cadet Grainger could see the admiral's face freeze for a few seconds, then the inevitable confused look. "What the hell just happened, Cadet?"

He waited before responding; the slightest sardonic smile on his face. "That, Admiral Shan, was our Visitors..."

She sat frozen. Cadet Grainger took advantage of the silence. He began working the shared recording that was linked to both of their comms. He manipulated the recording to go to a moment of the brilliant flashes—where even the shadows of the township's bulbous buildings were stretched out by several yards, due to those flashes of lights! He then let the still image slowly play back...indeed, so slow, that Admiral Shan could finally see several structures *within* the lights!

"My word," was all that she said; her eyes wide-opened.

"We wouldn't have discovered them without the station's Sentient. It tried to tighten up the vid, so we could get a better understanding of the objects, but they were simply too fast and the light too brilliant...Sentient clocked them at 198,000 miles a second—"

"That's the same reading that Director Tuun's team had measured on one of the recordings we viewed... right before they all vanished and the recordings blanked out!"

"Exactly, Ma'am..."

Admiral Shan took a few seconds to do a little calculating. "Well, you know what that means, Cadet Grainger: first of all, given what our Sentient has discovered for us, it's safe to say that these phenomena are *not* natural. *And* given our Visitors are traveling a bit *faster* than light-speed—"

"It means they are strategically hitting us at certain points...otherwise, at the rate they were traveling they would've made it to Erth several days ago!"

"Right..." She was nodding at that point; deep into the sciences that the Sol Governance had taught *all* its political officials. "That would make sense *why* that automaton was able to record all this, and for them to even continue to function at all!"

"Well, in *that* case, Admiral, it shows a *weakness* on the Visitors' end... given that we *know* they disrupt *all* recordings while they abducted our people, it stands to reason they *should* have taken out all those automatons on Pluto near Tombaugh; since they also have visual recording!"

Admiral Shan was nodding excitedly at that point; glad to see the Governance had some kind of advantage...in the old days, it was called 'home field advantage.'

Now Admiral Shan's eyes inquisitively looked upon Cadet Grainger's image on her comm. "All the same, have you all continued to try to reach *Justifier*?"

"Yes, Ma'am. We tried several times with no results."

She simply nodded in turn. They both sat quietly; looking at the looped-recording of that scene the cadet had shown to the admiral.

"Cadet," Shan finally said after their long, pensive thoughts, "excellent work! Now I'm going to need you and whoever's available to help set up *another* emergency meeting with the Members!"

"Ma'am!"

And the link was disconnected.

CHAPTER 10

Hours after Admiral Reshma Shan had her meeting via comm-link with Cadet Shawn Grainger, she met with the Sol Governance's Members once again. *This* time, with the information Cadet Grainger had revealed to her, the meeting went a lot better for the Admiral about 'the Visitors'—a nomenclature that simply stuck in all the discourse among the Governance's officials and its ranks.

Indeed, between those two meetings of the Members and each Member's respective agencies or companies, the Governance was able to come up with a working plan to combat that FTL-tech enemy.

With the newly-installed garrisons at *every* distance-markers in the Sol system, the Governance Council would "deputize" Members' citizens and company workers in the region *within* Saturn, Jupiter, and the Asteropia asteroid belt, so that every individual had the legal authority to carry weapons on their person at all times, with the understanding that such enactment by the Governance was temporary. The deputization would end when the threat of the Visitors was over, or close to ending, at best. Given the movements of the Visitors was just beyond that region, having citizens give succor to the Governance's military was like doubling the Governance's defense forces for *free*. There *were* objections by several Members of the Governance's body, but given the situation with the Visitors there was not enough time to debate the deputization plan...at least, that's what the Governance's Council Chair, Xi Zehan, *said* was the reason. It was well-known that she, and many other Members of the body, had always been biased *for* 'weaponizing' Sol's citizenry as a whole! Other presented plans by Xi for legislating such policy were defeated several times in the Council's procedures in time past. But *now*, given the threat from the Visitors, most had anticipated success of her deputization bill.

There was nothing like the threat of a foreign or *alien* aggressor to galvanize such nationalistic legislation in a government's body...

Also, the Governance would deploy a relatively new weapon designed by its scientists a few decades prior. The Centralized Collider was based on the principles of the old atom-smasher technology of the 20th and 21st centuries. Generally speaking, the only main difference was instead of needing nearly 20 miles of a small tunnel to sling atomic particles around and crashing them together to get energy and information, the

Centralized Collider was able to do *that* from a single output...the particles were shot out of a nozzle that had several nano-outputs and were all concentrated into a single spot and the *same* collision would occur as an atom-smasher! Governance scientists were able to adjust the size of the collision from that of a tiny firecracker to the obscene scale of a nuclear bomb! The Governance, however, tightly controlled and legislated what institutions were able to use the Colliders at *that* magnitude! Indeed, it was illegal in all of Sol system for individuals *not* associated with an institution to even use a Centralized Collider.

Given that the Governance already had existing Colliders stationed throughout Sol, it was the hopes of the Council that such weapons redeployed—quickly!—throughout the Sol system from Saturn to Erth-proper space would at the very least slow down the encroaching Visitors...

It had been several days since Admiral Shan had a virtual-meeting with the Council Members of the Governance board, and there was, literally, no news regarding the Visitors coming from the outer regions of the Sol system. The island of Pacificalis was placed on emergency status, along with the headquarters of the Governance, itself. All of the capitals, major metropolitan regions, and military facilities on planet Erth were, also, locked into emergency mode, thanks to the myriad of Council Members of the Governance.

Admiral Shan and her team finally got a lead on the Visitors *and* got backing from the solar system-wide government, and the Visitors had *now* decided to go 'radio silent,' as that very old phrase went. It was suspicious to the admiral. As if someone had told the Visitors that Humanity had finally built up a defense against them and they decided to hold back from invading the rest of Sol system! Shan decided to contact her old friend, Doctor Urla Franks, and see if she could help her from a more scientific approach.

The two women decided to meet at one of Pacificalis' Physical Universities. With Dr. Franks' connections as one of Governance's scientists, she was able to secure an entire auditorium for them. Given that the whole Island was in a state of emergency, there weren't many students around the University to get in the way. Those few around were given special exception, most likely because they were affiliated with Governance's military or University structures in some way. There, they began to use the classroom's media kiosk to further investigate the situation with the Visitors.

"I don't like it," the admiral said as she blew out a sigh. She had slumped into a nearby seat in the audience front row section of the auditorium. Like Dr. Franks, she had a beat-up cup with coffee in it. Compliments of a merchant-friend with a café near the

University grounds. "Maybe they were monitoring our communications and found out our plans?"

Dr. Franks gave a tacit nod; her lined face pinching. "Given their advanced technological abilities, it would be irresponsible to *not* consider that..." The scientist thought more on their little meeting, which had gone on for over an hour at that point. She couldn't help but notice from the corner of her eyes that Shan was staring at her. "What's on your mind, Admiral? I haven't seen you look at me like that since we *first* met!"

That, of course, caused Admiral Shan to look away. She thought for a few more seconds. "I *just* noticed your robe..."

Dr. Franks sat still, waiting to hear more from the middle-aged woman, whom was a little more than ten years her junior. "And," she said with a laugh.

"And...honestly, it reminded me that there are rumors that you are of Tellmondonian heritage."

At that point, Franks sighed impatiently. Now she, also, took a seat on the front row; two seats over from her friend. "Urla...look, I've been dealing with this issue of my ethnicity since before you were born, young lady!" They both laughed. For *young*, the admiral was not! "Honestly, I'm not completely sure myself. My family has a lot more pictures of robed relatives from time past compared to other people's families, I'll grant you that. But..."

Dr. Franks' eyes drifted toward the kiosk, with all its projected telemetry, images, and winking lights. "Reshma, it's been about a hundred years since many of the Tellmondonians had migrated to the asteroid field and re-established their colony out there! From articles I've read about them *and* the few Tell's I've actually met, it's safe to say that the majority of Tellmondonians are in the Asteropia development!"

"Doesn't mean you are *not* Tell', though."

"True...I admit, when I've seen my older relatives when I was much younger, most of them always wore robes, had long hair, and a lot of them tended to have that lanky body-type that Tell's often have."

"Because of the lower-gravity from Asteropia's artificial gravity in their cities," Admiral Shan input as she straightened up in her seat.

"That's it...I find it interesting and ironic at the same time, that at some point, most of those who traverse the solar system have either gone through, or stayed at Asteropia's asteroids. Given Humanity's complex history of conflicts between different cultures, I'm guessing there are a lot more Governance citizens *with* Tellmondonian blood than they'd like to admit!"

Now it was Admiral Shan's turn to subtly nod. "Well, you know *I* don't care about such things. But of all the years

I've known you, I don't remember ever asking you."

"Let's face it; the Tell's haven't been the kindest whenever I've visited the asteroid field and some of the Tell's' cities. We've all heard complaints about their attitudes toward Governance citizens...and I *look* Tellmondonian!"

Both laughed. Shan took a gulp of her coffee. Neither said anything for a while. Partially taking a break from their intense brainstorming session to deal with the Visitors; partially because the subject of Tellmondonians was *still* controversial for Sol citizens, even in the 23rd century! Most Sol citizens—especially those on Erth—yet blamed the ancestors of the Tell's for leaving Erth back in the 1990s and secretly setting up an underground colony of millions on the Moon! It was complicated enough that the Tell's had colonized Erth's moon clandestinely, given the various governmental and private space-powers of the 21st century, back then, had run-ins with the Tellmondonians. But most importantly, scientists of the day had discovered that all the human development on such a small, astronomical body as Erth's moon had corroded its geological structure and caused the Moon to actually *recede* toward Erth!

Given the pull of Erth's gravity on such a 'hollowed out' moon, it was the absolute worse environmental catastrophe Humanity had ever experienced! Fortunately, the space-powers of Erth of the mid-21st century had gotten their scientists together with those of Tellmondo, and they were able to *stop* the Moon's recession toward Erth...it took about 20 years, and millions upon millions of metric tons of mined erth shipped out to the Moon for patching, but the Lunar Recovery Project worked! Even during the days of Admiral Shan and Dr. Franks of the early-23rd century, Erth's moon was about one-third the distance it was from Erth *before* the

Lunar Recession! The Moon loomed larger in the sky than what the human species had evolved to know it—even during the mornings! And Humanity had strictly banned *any* development on the Moon perpetually.

It was this deep space history that had worked against Tellmondonians in the Governance's solar government of 2217. And for Dr. Urla Franks, specifically.

"When was the last time you've been to Asteropia anyway," Admiral Shan asked as she drank the last of her coffee.

Dr. Franks had to think for a moment. "Seven...maybe eight years ago?"

"My goodness! Why so long?"

A shrug from the elder woman. "I've gotten older...to travel so far out from Erth anymore is harder for me, despite our record-speed vehicles over the past few decades. Plus, ever since Chustin died, it's not quite the same."

At that point, the admiral felt guilty for asking her last question.

"Do you think they're examining them," Dr. Franks asked; jolting Shan back to the business at hand.

This time it was the admiral that needed time to think. "With the limited information we have on the Visitors at this stage, impossible to tell. As bad as this might sound, I *hope* that's the worst it!"

The scientist made a wincing face. "You know, Reshma, I've *never* been comfortable with that name we've been calling them: *Visitors*! So benign..."

By that point, Admiral Shan had gotten up and tossed her empty coffee cup into the recycler in the auditorium. She walked up to the looming kiosk; looking at one of the looping-images they had of the Visitors, taken from one of those mining automatons on Pluto. The replaying recording showed some hidden craft cloaked in flashes of light. "Well, none of us have exactly had a social with them and found out what they preferred to be called. So..."

"I suppose *aliens* would be a bit too clichéd, then," Dr. Franks put to her sardonically.

CHAPTER 11

ABOARD THE PLANETARY WATCH STATION, NUMBER 2; THE ASTEROPIA REGION...

"...This is not a practice-run...Watcher 2 personnel, man your stations... This is not a practice-run...Watcher 2 personnel, man your stations..."

The automated alarm of Watcher 2 turned the whole interior of the asteroid-sized station into a blaring red facility! After so many minutes, the masculine auto-voice stopped, but inside the entire station the red lighting remained the duration of whatever emergency the station faced. This was a standard operation aboard all seven of Sol system's planetary watch-guards; even Watcher 7, which was based on Pluto's largest moon, Charon. The hexagonal, planetoid-like station also flashed red on the outside, should, for whatever reason, the soldiers stationed on nearby asteroids or those flying in their tactical ships missed the transmitted alarm!

"Sentient," Director Robert Baptise addressed the station's computer nerve-center as he rushed to his own station, "make sure all of this is recorded! Bosses at Pacificalis made it a point to ensure that we get better images of our enemy...we can't know how to defend ourselves from them if we don't know who and what we're dealing with!"

"Yes, Director Baptise," the Sentient responded; the same voice as that of the alarm.

Director Baptise quickly looked around the command suite, making sure everyone was stationed at their position. Standing at his terminal, he, then, engaged its telemetry. The command chamber was filled with officers relaying information to each other and to the director on the trajectory of the Visitors, how many troops were available for the battle, and how many of the space-issued Centralized Colliders were at the director's fingertips.

"Director," one of the officers in the communications section called out amid the flurry, "Commander Assan from the Asteropian auxiliary base is on-comm!"

"Open," Director Baptise commanded while bringing up relevant data on the situation.

The projected image of the commander of the Governance's headquartered-base within the Asteropian asteroids was small. The contact was meant only for Director Baptise.

"Robert," the young woman said perfunctory; her head swiveling as she talked, due to her base's *own* activities, "they've already taken out *half* our Colliders!"

A few officers working close to Baptise's station glanced at one another with absolute fear!

"Bloody hell," the director responded; freezing on the spot for a few seconds.

"They just flashed into Asteropia out of nowhere and broke off into what I can only call teams," Commander Assan stated as she gestured commands to her officers that were out of the line of sight.

"That's what the first report on them out of Pluto said they did. I'm activating the whole damn field troops, Etnah...and Etnah—*both* of our teams will have to throw the whole house at them, and if *that* doesn't work, we'll go ol' Morning Glory on them...you got that?"

"Understood, Sir," the commander said; her voice clearly not sounding enthusiastic about the likelihood of having to self-destruct her base! The comm-line was then cut.

Those same officers working nearby Director Baptise were *also* not thrilled about the 'Glory' option, either. Baptise could see it out of the corner of his eyes, but he had a job to do.

"Cornwell," the director called out to his second-in-command; whom was at the weapons bank, "all those Colliders set?"

"Already synchronized and tracking those bastards, Sir!"

Baptise snapped his head out of approval. He, then, punched into his communications to broadcast to the entire planetary Watch station. "All personnel manning Colliders are to strike Visitors upon immediate detection...should our defensive posture not work Watcher 2 will engage Morning Glory option...Baptise out!"

As soon as the director closed off his communications-link to the entire station, the sounds of high-powered guns were heard loading photonic-missiles!

Even in the heat of battle, everyone in the command chamber froze. And all eyes were on Director Baptise... two of those officers that worked adjacent to the director, whom showed disapproval in his commands, each had those guns trained right on his head from behind!

During the complete silence, the comm-system still blurted out other soldiers' communications within Watcher 2 and those out in the field inside their fighter spaceships. Some were awaiting a response from Director Baptise. He slowly turned around to see who was causing the confusion.

"Tauch, Voltma," he said after a sigh of disappointment. "Come on, guys...you see what we're up against! Look, when we all signed up to join Governance's military we all knew that the Glory option was—"

"We are acting on behalf of Respect Hausa," Commander Marcus Voltma threw out to him.

There were reactions of gasps and disgust throughout the command center. For a 'Respect' was a person of the highest authority within the Tellmondonian culture! Plus, Respect Hausa's politics were well-known throughout Governance-space and they were antithetical to the solar system-wide government! In a word, Lieutenant Claudia Tauch and Commander Marcus Voltma were old-fashioned *spies* for a *very* old enemy in the chess-game of solar system-wide politics!

"Why are you Governance people so anxious to risk blowing up parts of the asteroid field and send a storm of debris that would *kill* hundreds of thousands of *our* people? For that matter, thousands of Governance citizens, too, since we're so close to Mars!"

"Commander Voltma," Director Baptise came in, forcefully, "or whoever the hell you *really* are, do you understand the magnitude of our enemy?"

"The Respects of Advisory and *their* scientists have *also* been tracking the Visitors, Director Baptise," Voltma informed. It had, in fact, caught all the Governance officers off-guard! "And so far, the only thing we know for certain about Them is they have *not* killed a single person up to this point! Not *your* people in the Pluto region; not *your* special ops crew from *The Justifier*; and they won't kill us *now*..."

Despite themselves, the Watcher 2 station officers *and* Director Baptise seemed to be coming around to the spies' point! Indeed, the reports filed by the Governance officials did *not* officially list the Governance personnel as deceased. Just missing!

This time, Lieutenant Tauch came in; lowering her gun slightly; her face bright in countenance. "Look, there's no need for Commander Assan and her people in the auxiliary base— nor *you*—to kill yourselves over the blessed Visitors because you don't understand them!"

Many of the officers in the command chamber glanced at one another with alarm!

"Excuse me," Director Baptise said tersely.

Voltma, apparently the one in control between the two—even though Tauch had a higher position within the Governance's structure— held out a hand. "We don't have time to explain this to them, my Sister... Director Baptise; I'm asking you to please tell Commander Assan to stand down. I promise you, you'll see you have nothing to fear."

The director looked around the command center at his crew as the comm-link went wild with Governance soldiers trying to figure out why they could not reach their leader! Some in the chamber shrugged; some were a bit more apprehensive.

Voltma looked at Tauch, gave a quick nod with a smile, and they both dropped their guns and held up their hands in surrender. Director Baptise took a few more seconds of thought, then nodded to his communications team to contact Commander Assan. At first, she protested, but then relented upon hearing Baptise, himself, assuring it was true.

There still were voices coming over the comm-line. Most of them, now, were cursing due to the change in course!

"The Visitors will be here soon," Tauch warned as she looked between the director and her cohort.

The director decided to put out the fire before it spread. "Open comm, Burke...station-wide!"

The young cadet pushed a couple of buttons. "Comm's yours, Director."

"Baptise, here...we've had unexpected information come our way...be advised and stand by...all ships, hold your positions...all personnel manning Colliders, stand down—from what we've heard in the office, they don't seem to do any good against the Visitors, anyway...await my orders. Baptise out."

CHAPTER 12

SOL GOVERNANCE'S HEADQUARTERS. PACIFICALIS ISLAND...

The emergency situation with the Visitors meant that Admiral Shan was pretty much grounded on the island of Pacificalis. Several days ago she was scheduled to be on the continent of Europe for a conference on global economics and its ties to the solar system-wide politics of the Governance. Such a heady subject also included the military, given how a populace adversely behaves when that population does not have basic needs. But before that, she had just finished a weekly meeting for Governance top officers...*that* was when she first learned of the Visitors from Cadet Grainger. Her life, indeed, the entire solar system, was never the same after that.

Director Morelli Tuun and his crew out in planetary station Watcher 7 on Pluto's moon of Charon; Captain Joden Modune and his elite team from *The Justifier*, in the municipal base of Tombaugh on Pluto; and, *now*, Director Robert Baptise and his crew out on station Watcher 2—the closest abductions to Mars and Erth by the Visitors yet! There had been, yet, another virtual meeting of the Governance's Members after Director Baptise's and his people suffered the same fate as the two other Governance groups. The abduction of the *90-thousand-plus* military installation of Watcher 2 was all-together different from the others! Even by 2217, humans had not settled the region of space around Pluto that much. The watch station, Number 7, on Pluto's moon Charon, was staffed with only a few thousand personnel for the very reason of Pluto's neighborhood being sparsely populated and extremely distant from Sol's core. But an entire asteroid-sized base, with a crew of nearly 100-thousand? And *all* abducted in, literally, a matter of *seconds*...?

But there *was* something a bit different in the Watcher 2 abductions besides the population size...the space station's Sentient recordings went blank like the other abduction-events, but before they did, the vids throughout the station showed that Watcher 2 was in battle-mode! Director Tuun's crew in the land station on Charon were the first abducted, and, hence, the team's posture in the vids suggested that they were not in battle-mode. As for Captain Modune's non-declared mission aboard *The Justifier*—sent to scout out Tuun's situation—*their* recordings showed them in a more investigative posture. Of course, the vids also had the audio and telemetry to go with the images, so it went beyond mere guess-work. But when all the recording instruments blank out simultaneously throughout a whole base, it was still hard to construct exactly the context of events.

Indeed, another difference with space station Watcher 2 was its own records. The vids did have Watcher 2's crew called to station-wide alert, but this time the records were "cut," versus a simultaneous blanking out like the situation with Watcher 6 on Pluto and the *Justifier's* crew! In the last meeting Admiral Shan was in, they had come to the conclusion that someone had *manually* disengaged the recordings in station Watcher 2. Someone with knowledge of the asteroid-sized space station's comm-systems and artificial neural-network...the records had *stopped* up to the time that Director Baptise had been contacted by Commander Assan of the branch-base on one of The Asteropia's asteroids.

Even the 2D records had abruptly stopped. Later, both holographic and 2D records blanked out as one continued watching.

It was a change in the patterns, in regards to the Visitors phenomenon. To Admiral Shan, that could either be a good sign, in that the Sol Governance's defenses were working aginst the Visitors. *Or*, perhaps, they were simply adapting to the Governance's fight against them...

The admiral was going from one meeting to another. She decided to grab a snack from one of the food-kiosks when she got a call from Cadet Lisa Watson.

"Cadet Watson," Admiral Shan responded tautly as she unsheathed her snack and looked at the device; walking through a crowded lobby and toward a floor-lift, "make it quick...I'm about to meet with—"

"Respect Hausa wants to speak with you," the young woman said, almost furtively. "And *you*, only, Admiral!"

By that time, the admiral had stopped in the lobby. She thought for a long time as she chewed her snack. "Why the hell does he even want to meet with Governance people at all? He *still* thinks of the Governance as one big, solar system octopus with Erth as its head!"

The cadet was shaking her head. "Don't know, Ma'am...he said he's on the Island."

That caused Shan to jerk with surprise! "You mean, on Pacificalis...*now*?"

"Yes, Ma'am! In fact, I have him on-wait for you...I figured, it must've been important enough!"

As if we didn't have enough to worry about, the admiral thought as she quickly swallowed the last of her snack. "Well, where is he?"

"I'm sorry, Admiral, I didn't—"

"It's ok, Watson...patch him through, but I want you to tag our conversation *before* you disconnect from the line... just in case."

"Understood, Ma'am."

The monitor of Admiral Shan's device winked from the young cadet to an image of an old man, around his seventies; his face etched with time, and his hair cut short, but for a very long braid that was decorated with beads and wrapped around the Respect's thin neck...the nationalistic Tellmondonian that Respect Hausa was, he kept with the cultural traditions of the Tell's from Erth's moon from more than 220 years since its inception in the early days. A time when several of Erth's counter-cultures had banded together with their wealth and resources to clandestinely build a brand new world deep under Luna's regolith.

"Dayshine, indeed, Admiral Shan," came the voice of a cultured man, despite his tribal look. It came across as contrived, especially given his conflicting history with the Governance. The greeting was from the time of near-ancient space age travels; when the society of Tellmondo was founded deep within the surface of Erth's moon. Back then, Tellmondo's citizens stumbled into the habit of the salutation, upon periodically going to the Moon's surface and seeing natural sunlight. The cultural practice continued, long after the Tell's established permanent lighting in the city-sized, underground cave.

"Respect Hausa," she replied professionally, despite herself. "This is highly unexpected...I can only assume you are contacting me because it has something to do with the Visitors—"

"Ahh, yes...our blessed Visitors." He said this with no irony. Word had gotten around the solar system that *most* of the Tellmondonians had *favorably* viewed the arrival of the Visitors! Indeed, some had seen them as deities; others had seen the Visitors as messengers from a god or gods...a few of the Tell's were a bit more agnostic in the whole phenomenon.

"Forgive me for pulling you away from your tasks, Admiral," he went on.

"But, as is the case for most things political, you are the person in position who acts upon the Governance's policies. Time is of the essence, and I did not want to waste time in contacting the more senior Members of the Council."

"Well, I can certainly understand that...I was told you are on Pacificalis," the admiral said as she scooted herself to the side of the lobby; getting out of the way of running cadets and officers and others in walking-meetings in the lobby.

"Indeed...the spaceport. As you have guessed, my business, here, is vital and I think will be helpful in dealing with our blessed Visitors."

Admiral Shan had a thought. "You couldn't simply had called me on a secured communique?"

The Respect shrugged a bit as he made a face. "I suppose I could have. But what I was given can only be appreciated in person, dear Admiral."

Admiral Shan froze. "Respect...were you given something by the Visitors?"

"Yes..." She waited to hear more information from him. But the elderly man gestured with the jutting of his chin that there were others with him off-vid. "I think it would be best if you came and met us out here, Admiral Shan."

She thought for a bit. Respect Hausa had a reputation in the solar system for being a bit odd in personality, but everyone knew him to be a no-nonsense kind of person. He would not have trekked all the way from the asteroid field to Erth if he had not felt it was necessary.

"Where in the spaceport are you," she finally said; regretting that she would have to re-arrange, yet, another meeting due to something else coming up.

"One of the private hangars, closer to the outer perimeter... nine-point-four."

She was nodding her head. "Ok, I'll have to do a bit of arranging first. And I don't want people to recognize me.

The public and other officers might get panicked if they see an admiral rushing about in the spaceport!"

"That would be wise, Admiral Shan... until then."

After his image blinked from her comm-device, Admiral Shan called up Cadet Watson. "Cadet, did you record my conversation with the Respect?"

The admiral could see the young woman refer to a terminal bank to her side, then look back up. "We got it, Admiral."

"Good. Share it with all of the Council Members—I don't want to get chewed out for not getting them involved soon enough, like the first time with the Visitors! Then have First Lieutenant Hu contact me...I want her to assemble a small team and meet me at our main hangar. And, Watson...tell Hu and the others to dress in their street clothes."

Shan could tell the cadet wanted to ask why, but she was trained enough to simply confirm the order and contact Cadet Grainger.

CHAPTER 13

PACIFICALIS SPACEPORT;
HANGAR 9.4...

Like most spaceports of the 23rd century, Pacificalis' port was right on the edge of the city-island, and most of the lanes, runways for the planetary skyporters, and landing-pads for the spaceships wrapped around the entire city itself! It was a fundamental change from the old days of sky-flight of the 20th and 21st centuries when most airports were built on the outskirts of a metropolis. Modern day designers assigned different segments of the ringed-spaceports to various destinations, that way skyporters and spaceships were in far less of a chance in crashing into each other or causing too much of a traffic jam.

Admiral Shan, First Lieutenant Tanya Hu, Lieutenant Fred Greyson, and Cadets Marla Pointe and Shawn Grainger, all donning civilian clothes typical of a tropical environment setting, walked quickly from the rented civilian land vehicle that was automatically stowed within one of the spaceport's hangar transport facility. Hangar 9.4 was in a section of Pacificalis' spaceport system that was more for industrial clients— various Erthen governments, private corporations, and such. The sector lacked the show-biz of the main parts of a typical passenger spaceport or skyport, with all their vendors, cultural attractions, and knots of people traversing or lounging around...

Admiral Shan, with a large-rim hat obscuring most of her head, craned her neck to find the right building. She saw a couple of young men, dressed in typical Erthen civilian-ware, walk up to them from another vehicle stowage building. One of them nodded at Shan's team, and the two began to walk in another direction. Shan's small team glanced at one another for apprehension, but followed, nevertheless.

The two men led the Governance team to the back area of an older structure of the spaceport, where spare parts for spaceships and sky-vehicles were stored. And there was something else in the midst of those old pieces of equipment...something that was casting long, stretching shadows in the old, darkened facility, with light so bright, it still hurt to look upon it even *with* sunglasses on! Which all five of the Governance operatives had on, anyway, given the sunny climate of the region near the Marshall Islands.

Respect Hausa was standing about seven feet from it when Admiral Shan's team walked up to the large chamber of the facility, but all five halted at the doorway upon fully seeing the

Object! The two young men joined the Respect and stood next to him— guards, most likely. All three men shimmered in the exuding light! The loosely-spherical, shifting glow had alternated, and its luminosity slightly pulsated...there were swarms of dust-like particulates whizzing about the whole phenomenon, but looked something like air-borne ember; as if from a campfire! The core of the phenomenon was around five feet off the floor of the chamber. The very center of the event was so bright, one had to shield their eyes from it—again, even with sunglasses on! There was actually the smallest of some audible sound coming from It. Almost more like the *feel* of a percussion, versus the *sound* of it!

"It's safe, dear Admiral," the Respect called out. "Trust me...we, Tell's, have been studying the Visitors *longer* than the Governance has! The worst anyone has ever gotten from it is a serious tan!"

The two young men accompanying Respect Hausa laughed.

"Yeah," Admiral Shan came back sardonically, as her team looked on, "and if one is not careful with suntans, they could turn out cancerous! Do you think it's such a good idea to be so close to that Thing?"

At that point, Respect Hausa simply walked over to the Object, slowly reached out with one of his thin, wiry arms while his hand was in a pinching motion—and the whole phenomenon was gone! And along with the living light, its accompanying "feeling!"

He, then, carefully turned to face the Governance crew while he safely maintained his hold on something. "All that...was generated from *this* tiny piece of technology, about the size of an apple seed!"

By that time, the Governance team had joined the Respect and his two companions in the chamber. For the longest time, no one from Shan's team said anything. They just looked at the elliptical Object between the elder's forefinger and thumb. A couple of the Governance crew had the slightest of smiles, but the other three were stoic; including Admiral Shan.

"So, what happened to our people," the admiral finally asked, crossing her arms.

Respect Hausa seemed disappointed with the Governance team's reaction. After sighing, he turned to the two young men behind him. One of them had produced a reinforced container a mere few inches in size. It was opened and the Respect placed the alien Object into the padded interior of the container, and the guard shut it and walked off to place the Object somewhere out of Shan's sight. Hausa then turned to face the admiral.

"All these millennia that Humanity had wondered if there were not only other life in the universe besides Erth—but *intelligent* life! *You* finally see something apart of that intelligent life-force, and what do you do? You reduce the experience to some damned checklist from a military exercise!"

"None of this matters if the Visitors abducts our people, Respect!"

Both voices had echoed in the chamber. Indeed, that same "percussion" feeling had washed over all eight humans in the chamber right after Admiral Shan's elevated sentence had ended! Where ever Respect Hausa's guard put the fortified container with the Seed, it had not mattered; *everyone* had felt the Seed's "displeasure." That caused all five of the Governance crew to freeze and stare at one another with widened eyes! Their eyes, then, went back onto Respect Hausa. Whom was laughing at this point, and his two guardians smiled.

"Yes, our blessed Visitors *know* when we, humans, are being aggressive, and I don't think they rather like it!"

"Permission to speak, Admiral Shan," Cadet Grainger said excitedly. He and

First Lieutenant Tanya Hu were the two Governance crew who seemed to appreciate the Object more than the others.

Admiral Shan thought for a few seconds. Cadet Grainger had always been a faithful, and very effective soldier. She gave him a firm nod. Grainger, then, turned to face the Respect, and pointed toward where the other guard had come back from when he moved the Object.

"Is that one of Them, Sir?"

"No...actually, the best that Tellmondonian scientists can guess at this stage is, apparently, these Seeds seem to act as some kind of probe *for* the Visitors! Almost like the way we, humans, had sent our own probes throughout the solar system. And, much like humans' planetary probes with Artificial Sentience, our scientists speculate that what these Seeds also do is act as ambassadors!"

There were snickers and sarcastic blows from the Governance crew.

Even Cadet Grainger seemed to have found *that* a bit much to swallow. The Respect sadly shook his head. He had always felt that Erthens from Sol's core region had lacked imagination and the ability to project possibilities.

"Listen, my friends...from what my subordinates in political offices have told me, Tellmondonians have been abducted by the Visitors *weeks* before your people out on Pluto were taken!"

"What," exclaimed Admiral Shan.

Even Respect Hausa's guards were silently nodding at his point. "Yes, Admiral. Given the Governance's and Tellmondonians' adversarial relationship over the past two centuries, I would say it makes it hard for Tell' scientists to share discoveries with our old enemies!"

The Governance team shared silent glances at one another. But the Respect thought more on his words.

"But," Hausa said more cheerfully as he slapped his thin, sinewy hands together and rubbed them, "we are *now*, literally, in the days of enlightenment! For our blessed Visitors have arrived and have already began to show us the way to a brighter form of conscientiousness...even I admit, I must work on my proclivity to hardline politics! I cannot lead if I do not follow the Visitors' way! So, no need to recount the skirmishes and wars between Erthen governments and the Tell's, huh?"

He then laughed and patted his guards on a shoulder.

Again, the Governance crew looked at one another, but this time with confusion and uncertainty.

"Uh, Respect," the admiral came in; carefully choosing her words, "how do you know *what* the Visitors want when they're aliens that, apparently, use a very different means of communication from us? And, quite frankly, Respect Hausa, I hope you're not implying that the rest of Humanity start to follow *you* just because your own government was the first to..."

The old man was giving her a devilish smile.

"Oh, blazes," the admiral exclaimed. She was thinking things through. "Respect...when you said Tellmondonian scientists had been observing the Visitors before the Governance..."

She whipped around to look at her crew of four. She could see it on Cadet Grainger's face—that he, too, understood what was going on! The others were still working on the problem in their heads. Admiral Shan whipped back around to look at the Respect. "Respect, please tell me you did not *steal* that Seed from your own government! Is that *why* you are here? Hiding from the Respects' Advisory Council?"

The Respect was already motioning before he even spoke. "Dear Admiral... it is not *stealing* when it involves aliens! What my fellow Respects were doing to the Seeds were an absolute blasphemy to the foundation of

111

ancient-Tellmondo's belief structure! We do not put our faiths in governments nor corporations, Admiral—"

"*You* abducted them *first*," Cadet Marla Pointe spoke out of protocol. Though the Governance crew were in civilian clothes to conceal their meeting with the Tellmondonian Respect, they were *still* on official Governance duty!

"Mind your mind, Cadet," the second officer of the small team, First Lieutenant Hu, scolded Cadet Pointe!

But Admiral Shan held up one of her hands without a word and nodded her approval. Cadet Pointe continued.

"That's why the Visitors are here in our solar system...at some point, Tell' scientists had discovered this Seed and the Respect Council agreed to quietly take the Seed—I'm guessing for good ol' fashioned experimentation!"

"And I'll bet you," Cadet Grainger, now, came in; after a nod from the admiral, "that the Seed had sent a distress signal! Maybe your scientists knew about it, maybe they didn't. And, *now*, the *blessed Visitors* have come to Sol to get their own Seed back!"

"And in the process," the admiral, now, finished up, "the Visitors took *our* own 'seeds.' As in, our fellow Governance people...is that what all this is about, Respect Hausa?"

The Respect and his two guards were not smiling at that point anymore. In the silence, Admiral Shan noticed Cadet Grainger mulling something over.

"We're pretty much on at-ease now, Grainger!"

The cadet thought, yet, even more before speaking. "The only problem with our thought-process is the Seed itself, Admiral...Ma'am, I just don't see the Visitors going through all this trouble for a supposed probe!"

Admiral Shan's eyes drifted away as she, too, thought further on the guess-work. Then..."You bastards abducted one of the Visitors' *children*, didn't you? That isn't a probe at all! It's some version of an infant—or, maybe even a fetus!"

Those in the Governance team that did not understand were, now, wide-eyed and slowly looked upon the Respect as if *he* were an alien himself!

"Oh, my god," Lieutenant Greyson said slowly; his head craned in the direction where one of Respect Hausa's guards had hidden the Seed.

Respect Hausa peered at his two aides. They looked dejected. Apparently there was no rebuttal to the Governance's operatives...apparently.

"Very good, dear Admiral," the Respect finally admitted. He tilted his head in the direction of the hidden Seed. "But there's only one problem with your deduction...*that* is not the only Seed!"

CHAPTER 14

The revelation that Respect Hausa of Asteropia had abducted, as it turned out, over a hundred of the Visitors' Seeds had completely changed everything about how the Council of the Governance would approach the Phenomenon, as it was often called, of the arrival of the Visitors! Of course, Admiral Shan would have to quickly set up another virtual meeting with the Members as soon as she and her small incognito crew made it back to Headquarters.

But before the admiral could worry about the meeting, she had to place Respect Hausa and his two guards, Astro'hope and Sahurell, under arrest! Her crew of four simply whipped out their hand-sized guns they had been hiding on their person, and commandeered the Respect and his guards with *their* guns that they, also, had hidden on them! The Governance operatives were legally obligated to arrest the three based on a few Governance laws, along with non-binding agreements with the Tell' society. Since there was no *official* political relationship between the Sol Governance and the Tellmondonians of Asteropia's asteroid field, the two societies got around that with unsigned, but *witnessed*, agreements... in the case of the arrest of Respect Hausa, it was based on the fact that *'Governance personnel with knowledge and the witness of the offender(s) with the illegal ascertainment of persons, and/or item(s) of significance...'*

As the Governance crew stripped the Tell's' guns from them, Admiral Shan made sure to document the whole episode. For the animosity between the Governance's Erth-based culture and the Tellmondonians living mostly in the asteroid field ran deep and long. She did not want to start an intra-solar war between the two sides, should Respect Hausa's arrest be interpreted as something of an infringement on Tellmondonian sovereignty! After all, Hausa *was* a Respect. Despite Tellmondo's societal philosophy of every citizen being on par with one another, the Respects of the Advisory Council *still* held a higher level of concern when it came to intra-solar conflicts.

And, then, there was the Visitors' Seed... Admiral Shan made sure *she* took care of transporting the reinforced case that contained the tiny, hard-surfaced Object! Shan had First Lieutenant Hu record her taking official Governance custody of the Seed as Shan recited legal codes while doing so. She had always felt funny doing that part of the job. She was not a particularly religious or spiritual person, but she had visited several theist institutions where they would chant as they part-took in ceremonial rituals. When she did the codified readings based on Governance's laws throughout her career, she always thought of those theist institutions.

After the admiral's team inconspicuously walked Respect Hausa and the two young Tell's through the industrial section of Pacificalis' spaceport, they placed the three men into the back of their land vehicle and drove back to Governance's headquarters. Just before the ride, Admiral Shan, taking Cadet Pointe with her for backup, hopped into the back of the large vehicle with the Tell's so she could convince the Respect or one of his guards to tell them *where* the rest of the Seeds were. The old man and his aides *politely* refused to disclose the location. That made Shan's job a lot harder. For, now, based on those same non-binding agreements between the Governance and the

Tellmondonians, she *had* to contact the Advisory Council on Asteropia!

All this, while Admiral Shan had to worry about *when* the Visitors would strike next...

"Admiral," one of the cadets from the command suite informed her in one of Governance's headquarters-halls, "the Prime Governor is here for the meeting."

"Thank you, Cadet Krickens," Admiral Shan said; exhaustion beginning to show on her face. She straightened her posture and made sure her dark uniform was in place. Prime Governor Henrick Valerio may have been a civilian and young enough to be Shan's son, but he was the chief of the entire Governance government!

Tall, slender, and dressed in traditional business attire, Prime Governor Valerio approached Admiral Shan as she stood next to the door of her official quarters so they could join the on-going virtual meeting with the Advisory body of the Tellmondonian

Respects. He was flanked by five body guards. One handed Valerio a briefcase; the Prime Governor nodded a *Thanks* to him. Those same five guards took positions right in front of the admiral's quarters, which was in a section of the Governance's headquarters where the halls were wide and posh...a reflection of the higher ranking Governance officials in that section of the base.

Admiral Shan and the prime governor shook hands and went right into her suite. During such emergency virtual meetings, it was against policy to have *any* aides amid the proceedings. So the hard work of keeping notes, working out logistics, and other practical things were incumbent upon each official attending.

The projected patch-work of tiny, three-dimensional head-shots of most of the several hundreds of Governance Members in the checkered format was up and running already. What was different was whenever there were guest-speakers in an official meeting *with* the Members, those guests' images were shown several inches off to the side *from* the large, holographic table that was projected a couple of feet off of the admiral's desk...that way, it was easy for the Members and said-guests to keep track whom they were speaking to.

Normally, Reshma just sat in her chair to conduct her meetings with the other Members. But Prime Governor Valerio just stood before the admiral's machine that transmitted their images before the others in the meeting. Not wanting to look lazy—especially as an *older* Member!—Admiral Shan, also, stood. Automatically, the machine transmitted Valerio's and Shan's faces within the projected, checkered tables of the Members and several Respects.

"Ahh, I see the prime governor has joined us," one of the Respects, Utopian's Rocks, announced; though unnecessary since the Sentient that ran the machine's program always alerted the other Members whenever someone else had joined in the conversation.

Several within the multi-boxed projection greeted Valerio. He, graciously, nodded back.

"Before you left to usher the prime governor in," Council Chair Xi Zehan, said, as she picked up the business, "Admiral Shan, you said that you and your people were not able to get any further leads to the location of the other Seeds from Respect Hausa..."

"That's correct, Chair Xi...I thought, perhaps, one of the distinguished Respects could help out in this regard. I've got a feeling that Respect Hausa would be more receptive if *another* Respect were to talk with him. It would save a lot of time...time, which we all need to prepare for *another* round of abductions or strike from the Visitors!" She gave a shrug, and the prime governor gave an approving nod.

"But, Admiral, he is no nationalist; he's simply a deeply spiritual man with a big following that's taken things too far," Respect Hannah'mondo informed. In her mid-fifties, she was one of the *youngest* of the Respects! "He has disciples all over the solar system; some are even *non*-Tellmondonians! These people have been colluding with him in kidnapping these Seeds! That last situation you all spoke of earlier, on your space station Number 2? There was word among Tell's that there were *several* of Respect Hausa's people that had infiltrated your station and had something to do with Watcher 2's abductions!"

"Considered *that* confirmed, by way of my several sources," Yavon Baker, prime minister of the United Kingdom, contributed.

"Ok," Admiral Shan said, "we know that Respect Hausa has disciples all over Sol, whom are willing to risk *other* humans' lives at the hand of the Visitors; all so he and his followers can abduct the Visitors' babies..." She shrugged again. "And do *what* with them? Trust me, fellow Members, my team and I went round and round with Respect Hausa *and* his guards. But they just *sit* there, in their separate cells...talking about the *blessed Visitors* and smile!"

For the first time, the entire grid of solar system powers actually fell silent!

"Admiral," this time it was the prime governor that contributed, "what did you do with the Seed that Respect Hausa had?"

All eyes in that giant, floating grid fell on her. She turned to address him directly. "Given the special circumstances of the Seed's status as both a political situation *and* a scientific one, I ordered for it to be placed into Governance's laboratory vault."

The prime governor and many of the Governance's Members were nodding in agreement with her choice. But the Respects, most scattered about the solar system just as the Members were, began to stir.

"With respect, Admiral," Respect Mores came in, "but you placed an *alien infant* in a vault?"

She smiled. "It's a vault designed to withstand a nuclear or fissionary bomb blast...without giving too much away, Respect, it was designed when the island of Pacificalis was first constructed nearly 70 years ago." Admiral Shan noticed that Prime Governor Valerio gave her a cautious look! "And that's about all I can tell you..."

"What if we took it out of the Vault and shipped it to open space and just let the Visitors take it," President Julio Raposa of Chile suggested.

There were boisterous agreements to Raposa's words. Council Chair Xi rapped her gavel!

"It would at least get them out of the region of space between Mars and Erth," Vornan Huntworth, the real estate tycoon with space station properties and other estates throughout the solar system, commented.

Again, more loud consent! And, again, more pounding from Chair Xi's gavel!

"Even if that were true," Admiral Shan came back in, "what about the rest of the Seeds we can't locate at this moment? I've got a feeling that the Governance giving *one* infant to the Visitors just won't satisfy them when there are at least a hundred more they're looking for!"

There were more tacit agreements on Shan's point.

"Well, we can't do *nothing*," the prime minister of Nigeria, Alkana Omalade, said. "If we cannot get the information of the whereabouts of the rest of the Visitors' children from Respect Hausa, then, perhaps we ought to conduct *raids* on his disciples and *take* the Seeds from the followers and give them back to the Visitors so we can all go back to our own lives!"

Absolute pandemonium...The Respects visiting in the virtual meeting had heard of the legendary

Governance proceedings, but this was the first time for most of them to have sat in on one! They gave very uncomfortable looks over the grid projection.

As Chair Xi continuously beat her gavel in a fruitless attempt to bring order to the Council's meeting, Prime Governor Valerio looked at Admiral Shan with a questioning face; wondering if Prime Minister Omalade had a good point, especially with so many of the other Members in agreement. She, in turn, gave a defeated shrug.

"Prime Governor," came the strong voice of Chair Xi after she had gotten order back into the meeting, "what is your opinion on this, Sir?"

He glanced back at Admiral Shan, then back at the holographic wall with the hundreds of faces looking right at him...

"I absolutely agree with Prime Minister Omalade, that we simply *cannot* suffer paralysis! Not when we could get hit with another round of abductions by the Visitors; and we cannot let Respect Hausa's disciples make things worse for all of us in the solar system by their careless actions! I say we vote on Member Omalade's motion!"

In the old days of governing on Erth, a system called Robert's Rules of Order was the given language of the day. The Sol Governance political machine was so vast, with the majority of Erth's governments being affiliated with it, the majority of the *thousands* of independent space habitats and stations affiliated as well, the various colonies on Mars and on several moons of other planets were a part of it, and pretty much all of human settlements scattered all the way out to the Pluto region... Such sprawling, meta-bureaucracy *required* a system of governing that was fluid!

Hence, since the founding days of the Sol Governance in the mid-22nd century, a more flexible version of Roberts Rules was adopted: once a Member simply *stated* an opinion on an issue, it was considered "a motion." After the prime governor's statement—by *new* Robert's Rules standards, a second of her motion— he called for the Council's Sentient to conduct the vote. And by a wide majority, the Sol Governance's Council voted on Prime Minister Omolade's motion and passed it.

The Governance's solar system-wide raids on Respect Hausa's disciples would begin, contingent upon the Governance's military officials' discretion.

This was where   Reshma Shan took control of that machinery of the solar system-wide government...

CHAPTER 15

With the Governance Council's authorization for the solar system-wide raids on *any* group or individuals associated with Respect Hausa, Admiral Shan, finally, had the legal and practical powers to go after Tellmondonians *and* non-Tell's that were always on the fringe of Sol society. They often came from the more intellectual quarters—the Physical Universities, the downtown cafés in the cities throughout Erth, many of the artificial habitats that freely floated between the zones controlled by Mars' space-powers and the regions of space close to the Asteropian asteroid field.

Oddly, those same educated citizens had followed Respect Hausa as if he were a cult figure! The movement saw the Visitors as near-divine beings that would bring Humanity to a level of Aquarius; where Tellmondonians *and* other humans throughout the solar system that were *not* ethnically Tell' could all co-exist. That was the good aspect of Respect Hausa's movement. As for the abduction of the Visitors' Seeds...

That very same day, after the Governance's Prime Governor Valerio showed up for the Members' virtual meeting with him and the Respects of Asteropia, Admiral Shan had convened a meeting with her core officers of the Governance. They already had been monitoring those very same Tell's and their sympathizers for years. So it was relatively easy, then, to connect which groups of them and individuals were actual *disciples* of Respect Hausa and which groups and individuals were simply *sympathizers* that did not take it as far as abducting the Visitors' Seeds...

Indeed, over the next several days that passed since the Members voted for the Sol-wide raids, the Visitors had struck again! *That* time, it was on a few of the developed asteroids within the Asteropian belt. Along with the accompanying pyrotechnics of the arrival of the Visitors, *Hundreds* of Tellmondonians had *flashed* out of Asteropia's cities and towns located within several asteroids! Admiral Shan's crew had guessed that the Visitors began to zero-in onto those who had kidnapped the Visitors' Seeds, and it was *their* turn, again, to grab from the humans! But, in the end, without any kind of context to the situation with the Visitors flashing about the Sol system, it was still just guesswork.

For that matter, Admiral Shan was *still* not completely sure about concluding that what they called "Seeds" really were the Visitors' offspring or not! The irony was it was *her*—Reshma Shan— during her reconnaissance to meet Respect Hausa at one of Pacificalis' spaceport's section, that had jumped to the conclusion that the tiny piece of metal-like object that the Respect had was a living being! Back then, it seemed like, to the admiral, that Respect Hausa was lying about the Seed, actually, being some probe sent by the Visitors. Lied, so he could trick Admiral Shan to believing that the Seed was just a probe?

That elusive question kept coming back to her: what did it profit Respect Hausa and his followers by abducting the Seeds? Whether or not the minute Objects were infants of the Visitors or, perhaps, some device? What was so important to the Respect and his 'Hausanite' disciples about the Visitors that they were all willing to get abducted *by* the Visitors or put into Governance prison for several years? And, of course, since *none* of them were talking to Governance authorities throughout the solar system, that made the system-wide raids necessary.

At least, to most *non*-Tellmondonians.

The raids were done quickly, relative to space-travel. Partially due to 23rd century high-speed ships; partially due to the redeployment of tens of thousands of Governance troops to most of those distance-markers scattered throughout Sol after Captain Modune of *The Justifier* and his team had zeroed-in on one of those markers, believing *it* to be some decoy of what Sol citizens later called the Visitors. The redeployment of so many troops as a blanket strategy was, at first, a controversial move by the Governance's Council chair, Xi Zehan. The monetary cost, the perception by many Sol citizens that those same troops could had been used for more day-to-day practical conflicts throughout the solar system...but with the new policy of the raids on Respect Hausa's disciples, the politics of that redeployment played well for Chair Xi, and there was talk of her, possibly, running to replace current prime governor, Henrick Valerio!

With the on-going raids of the Hausanites throughout Sol for over a week, by then, Admiral Shan was assigned a top-class war ship— *Gravity's Pull*! Or, colloquially, *Gravity*. It was one of the Governance's special space liners that were designed to virtually explode to its top speed in, literally, *three seconds*! So fast were those liners, the ships were able to escape *any* of Sol's planetary gravity wells in those three seconds...hence, *Gravity's Pull*.

The ship's thick anterior was one big blunt instrument that extended back about a thousand feet until the ship's backend sharply narrowed into a virtual sword! Such design was more for those occasions when *Gravity* traversed in the densest planets of the solar system, and aerodynamics were more of an issue.

Uptothatpointintheimplementation of the Raid policy, Governance troops had recovered over 50 of the 100 or so Seeds. In just over a week's effort, executed throughout the entire solar system, the on-going policy was considered a success! But none of that mattered until Admiral Shan and the Governance government found out a way to contact the Visitors and return their offspring back to them!

That line of thought had opened up questions as to *how* Respect Hausa and his disciples captured the Visitors' Seedlings to begin with! Of course, after the admiral had arrested Respect Hausa over a week ago on Pacificalis Island, she had already asked him that very question...he had either responded with a polite, 'I can't answer that,' or go into some speech about how the Visitors would impart their advanced societal ways upon Humanity! Hausa's two young body guards, Sahurell and Astro'hope, merely followed his lead. Admiral Shan had figured that the Respect and his Hausanites must have had some doctrine of action, because of the many disciples the Governance troops had detained in Sol, almost every one of them responded the exact same way that Respect Hausa and his two guards did when the admiral interrogated them at Headquarters!

Almost all of the disciples...

"She's who," Shan said, surprised that such an elderly man would even have a girlfriend at all, much less one in her twenties! The admiral was doing a daily check of the *Gravity*, making her rounds at each level. She had taken the 2D call on her comm as she kept her stride; looking about her crew and their ship.

"Respect Hausa's *girlfriend*, Ma'am," First Lieutenant Tanya Hu repeated furtively over the comm. The admiral had requested First Lieutenant Hu to be reassigned from Headquarters to work with her on *Gravity's Pull* since she was one of the closest staff to her. "And, Admiral...she's not even Tellmondonian!"

Admiral Shan shrugged to herself; yet walking her rounds of the ship. "That doesn't surprise me...isn't that what Hausa's all about: the brotherhood of Humanity and oneness with the blessed Visitors and all that... between you and I, Tanya, I'm actually sympathetic to his ideals! I just don't think humans should worship the damn things."

"No arguments from me on that point, Admiral!"

"Which team detained her," Admiral Shan asked while taking herself out of the main traffic area of the ship's walkway she was on.

"Cadet Jordan Tye, was the arresting soldier, Ma'am."

Shan thought for a second. "Isn't he from *our* ship?"

"That's the beauty of it, Admiral... she's in *Gravity's* detainment hall and she was just processed!"

They both shared a smile after First Lieutenant Hu linked an official Governance arrest picture of the young woman. She was disheveled from battling Governance troops from apprehending her. The telemetry identified her as Mary Brushwell; student at one of Mars' Physical Universities; from a middle-class background, her family originally from New York City back on Erth.

"Pretty," Shan said absent-mindedly. "How do we know she's telling the truth about being Hausa's primer?"

A shrug from Hu. "One of the other disciples detained told Cadet Tye, from what *he* told me...I suppose we could verify that during the interrogation phase. Ma'am, you'd be surprised how our team—"

"No," the admiral cut in after a thought. "I think I want to have a try at her... and I think I have just the friend to help back me up."

CHAPTER 16

ABOARD THE WAR-CLASS LINER *GRAVITY'S PULL*; NEAR-ERTH REGIONAL SPACE...

Doctor Urla Franks had gotten the call from her old friend, Admiral Reshma Shan, about voluntarily helping out with the interrogation of the Hausanite disciple Mary Brushwell. After the admiral had explained the situation of the detainment of Brushwell, and the University student's connection to Respect Hausa and his movement of abducting the Visitors' Seeds, Dr. Franks jumped at the opportunity! For she was one of those Governance citizens that was apprehensive about the arrival of the Visitors. She saw the aiding of Brushwell's interrogation as a chance for her to help fight against the aliens that had swept across the Sol system and abducted over a hundred-thousand humans!

In their communique, Admiral Shan was not shy to admit that she thought of Dr. Franks because of her reputation throughout the Physical Universities' solar system-wide network of intellectuals...Shan figured, the educated disciple of Respect Hausa, that came from the University of the physical properties of the universe, would find it a lot easier to talk with Dr. Franks than with *her*—an admiral, yes. But one of those practical people that did well at following orders and came up with some good ideas on her own from time to time...

The guard held up an index finger by the reinforced door's identifier. The single paneled door swooshed opened and the guard let the medium-height Mary Brushwell walk into the interrogation room. The door shut after Mary had cleared it. At the center of the decent-sized room were Reshma Shan and Dr. Franks. They sat next to each other at the sundry table; opposite of the empty chair that Brushwell would eventually sit.

"Hi, Ms. Brushwell," Shan started with a smile and an info devise in front of her, "I'm Admiral Reshma Shan of the Sol Governance military headquarters on Pacificalis Island." She gestured to Franks, next to her. "This is Dr.—"

"Urla Franks," the young woman said; her voice sauntering, "chief scientist of the energy conversion ratio of the Dark Matter Department... Erth-side."

Dr. Franks and Admiral Shan shared glances. Brushwell continued. "I attended a couple of your lectures on Mars, Dr. Franks."

That caused the scientist to finally smile. "Well, I hope you learned something...Mars is turning into one of the destination spots for the application of dark matter energies!"

"Yeah, it was one of my earlier course. But I ended up specializing in Modern Terraforming." Brushwell shrugged her small shoulders. "I figured, with those new programs that the Tellmondonians were offering students on Mars to help terraform some of their asteroids...why not?"

"Is that how you met Respect Hausa," Dr. Franks asked; poignant, yet soft enough as a conversation-piece.

Even Mary's laugh was young—almost like a little girl's giggle, in the ears of the older women. She pointed at the scientist as she nodded. "You're good, Dr. Franks...maybe *you* should be the cop here?"

The admiral and the scientist shared a genuine laugh.

"Ms. Brushwell," Shan came back in; voice accommodating, "I'm sure you understand the situation the whole solar system is in right now... As I understand it, you have a close relationship with Respect Hausa?"

The student was already nodding. "Yes..."

"Ok," Admiral Shan continued, "the way I see it, Ms. Brushwell, you have the opportunity to utilize your unique position in all of this, so people all around the solar system can get our family and friends back."

"I'm sorry, Admiral, but I think you have the wrong person in your interrogation chamber for that," Mary stated; direct but not terse.

The two older women shared concerned looks.

"Oh, no," Brushwell clarified, "I don't want to give you the wrong impression—"

"And what would that be, Ms. Brushwell," Admiral Shan said with a hint of anger.

"Well, that you and the Governance would think I would not be cooperative with you, in regards to our blessed Visitors' Seedlings!"

Admiral Shan was a bit agnostic on the Visitors' arrival to Sol. But Dr.

Franks, the *scientist*, had even *less* patience with the Hausanite disciples' deification of the aliens! Dr. Franks had to catch herself before she came across as condescending to Brushwell. She glanced at the admiral for permission. "Ms. Brushwell...what did you mean when you said we were interrogating the wrong person?"

Before answering, Brushwell sighed. "I know that Respect Hausa has a bit of an eccentric personality. I suppose it doesn't help when people see *me* with him out in public—especially the *non*-Tellmondonians from Erth, where there are still a lot of conservative people. I sometimes think because of those cultural differences, a lot of Erthens, in particular, are so biased against him..."

Admiral Shan and Dr. Franks glanced at each other; each with arched brows.

"Ms. Brushwell," Admiral Shan said, struggling to remain diplomatic, "I'm sorry, but we don't understand what you are getting at!"

"Hausa..." the student was slowly shaking her head, "he was not *abducting* the Visitors' Seedlings. He was *protecting* them *from* the Respects of the Advisory Board! He was only trying to *hide* the Visitors' Seeds!"

Just then, Admiral Shan remembered when she had arrested the Respect on Pacificalis Island, in one of the Island's spaceport divisions...just before she detained him, Respect Hausa had said something about how his fellow Respects and their scientists had committed a blasphemy against Tell' ethics with that one Seed!

Dr. Franks and Mary Brushwell both noticed how the admiral froze! Franks gave her friend an askance look.

"I have to admit," Admiral Shan said slowly, "Respect Hausa *did* say something about that...but..." Admiral Shan began to get a sick, sinking feeling in her stomach. *Was the Governance raiding the wrong group of people throughout the whole solar system?* "I thought the Respect was just trying to justify stealing the Seed from the Advisory Board!"

Brushwell gave the admiral a hardened look. "Like I said...biased against him!"

"Now wait a minute," Dr. Franks came back in; more defensive, "it's not like your fellow disciples and your boyfriend worked with Admiral Shan and the other officers of the Governance! From what I've heard in the media and prime sources, they simply would shut up; sing songs devoted to the Visitors...anything but answer the authorities!"

"That's because my brothers and my sisters felt it was *our* calling to protect the blessed Seedlings," Mary shot back. "I told you already: Respect Hausa gave his explanation to Admiral Shan; she had *already* made a judgement against him, and *now*, the blessed Seedlings have lost their protectors! And our blessed Visitors may be losing patience with Humanity!"

Admiral Shan snapped out of her dread of realizing the possibility of a *very* large injustice she may have been responsible for. "Ms. Brushwell...what do you mean, the Visitors may be losing patience with Humanity?"

Right in front of Admiral Shan and Dr. Franks, the University student seemed to have shrunk into a little girl...she fidgeted with her fingers as she looked at them. "Respect Hausa *senses* it...he told us, during some of our gatherings on Asteropia's asteroids...he warned us, after some of the Tellmondonian scientists had discovered some tiny, metallic Seeds out in the Kuiper belt region several months ago... Respect Hausa had warned the Tellmondonian Board to leave the Seeds where they were! But..."

Mary had started to endlessly shake her head.

"Oh, my god," Dr. Franks said with a very low, and worried voice. She said, nor did, anything else, except stared into a corner of the chamber.

Admiral Shan retrieved her communications device and called up her comms section of *Gravity's Pull.* "Sentient; Communications Center, this is Admiral Shan...I'm going to need a *top* emergency meeting with the prime governor and the Governance Council."

CHAPTER 17

ADMIRAL SHAN'S PRIVATE QUARTERS, ABOARD *GRAVITY'S PULL*...

"You mean to tell me that all those disciple freaks are *Protectors* of the Visitors' Seedlings," Prime Governor Henrick Valerio said with incredulity. He was met with the nodding of Admiral Shan's and Dr. Franks' heads. Dr. Franks was standing next to the admiral during the virtual emergency Council meeting.

Admiral Shan responded. "'Protectors of the Seeds,' is what *they* call themselves. We've been calling them Hausanite disciples, but..." She shrugged. "Anyway, we were able to confirm Ms. Brushwell's story with several other Protectors' stories. With the way we kept the detainees separated from one another, *and* how we did some story-switching to check for over-laps, I think it's safe to say what Ms. Brushwell is telling us is true."

There was a stirring among that rectangular honeycomb of the projected faces of the Governance Council. This time around, there were no Tellmondonian Respect guests for the meeting. Though it, certainly, pertained to them *and* their scientists!

Dr. Franks came in. "From what we're told—and it's the best we have to go on, right now—the Tell' scientists must have encountered something akin to the Visitors' *nursery* out in the Kuiper belt...one of those extremely distant planetoids floating about out there, where humans have probably never chartered from our scopes yet!"

"So," privateer space miner, Gustan Furvor, came in over the holographic grid, "those Respects we had in our meeting some time ago...were *they* responsible for all this trouble with the Visitors?"

"All those attending *that* meeting," Admiral Shan said as she nodded, "yes! Except one: Respect Aurora. From those same detainees we spoke with today, they *all* said, separately, that she was *not* in the faction of Respects that insisted on abducting the Seeds!"

"But she also wasn't on Respect Hausa's side, either," Prime Governor Valerio stated bluntly.

Shan's head snapped to the side as she thought on his statement. "Doesn't seem that way...but, the fact that she was *not* with the Respects for the Seed abductions is a plus, in my book!"

There were some voices of consent in the meeting.

"So," came Council Chair Xi, "what's the bottom line to *all* this, Admiral; Doctor? How do we give the Seeds *back* to the Visitors *before* they do, indeed, lose their patience with Humanity? Given their technological abilities to just to *abduct* over 90-thousand people from space station Watcher 2 *in mere seconds*, I'd hate to see their *weapons* capabilities!"

Now the meeting had erupted into chaos! Xi, due to her *own* words, had to gavel the attendees back to order! At that point, Admiral Shan and Doctor Franks looked at each other rather dubiously. That was not lost on the prime governor!

"Ladies...?"

Admiral Shan sighed and lightly clasped her hands together before speaking. "Now, for what it's worth, Members, it's a suggestion from Respect Hausa's primer, Mary Brushwell—whom is, I might remind you, a student at one of Mars' Physical Universities! So, I suggest we, at least, listen to her... Perhaps we ought to utilize what is already in place? As the ancient saying goes: Why re-invent the wheel?

"Since Respect Hausa and his Protectors of the Seeds disciples have been adept at *caring* for the

Visitors' Seedlings, maybe we should place Respect Hausa in charge of a Governance-mandated agency?"

By that time, there already were voices of opposition within the Council! But not everyone.

"An agency," the admiral continued, ignoring those voices, "with the charge of collecting however many more Seeds are at-large. May I remind you, the Governance's Raid policy has taken valuable time, given that the Hausanite disciples are *not* cooperative! Placing the very person that those disciples follow—with their *lives*, I might add, it might make sense to let Respect Hausa be the face of the replacement of the Visitors' Seeds..."

Still some disagreement from others in the Governance Council, but it had faded a bit! Admiral Shan had never stopped making the case...

"Upon collecting those Seedlings, have Respect Hausa's deputized disciples re-locate *all* the Seeds *back* to the Kuiper belt region, where the

Tell' scientists had stolen them from to begin with!"

Volleys of consent seemed to over-power those opposing the admiral's proposal. Which meant, in the lexicon of the Governance Council's system of legislating, a motion to enact Admiral Reshma Shan's concept...oddly enough, which, *also* meant that the Council would vote, indirectly, for the suggestion put by University student, Mary Brushwell!

But given the further gravity of the Phenomenon of the Visitors, yet, abducting *hundreds* or *thousands* of humans at a time, with the added sense that those *blessed Lighted Ones* had limited patience to get their offspring back, the Council voted to implement the 'Brushwell-Shan Policy!' Indeed, while the Governance's Sentient program conducted the voting, Chair Xi Zehan instructed the Governance Council to, also, vote on whether to rescind the Raid policy. Given that the policy had given powers to Governance military to enter and extract Respect Hausa's followers *without* need for a writ, the Council thought it counterproductive to maintain the ruling. A large percentage of the majority of the Governance Council voted to rescind the Raid policy. Effective immediately.

Indeed, the irony of *humans* enacting a law that gave powers to their military to abduct their own fellow citizens, while trying to fight off the abduction of humans from an *alien* civilization was well-observed by the solar system's media.

CHAPTER 18

ABOARD *GRAVITY'S PULL...*

It took a couple of days before Respect Hausa finally made it to *Gravity's Pull* from Governance headquarters on Erth. After the Governance's historic vote to rescind the Raid policy on Respect Hausa's disciples scattered throughout the solar system, the elder cult figure and his followers were *all*, now, considered legally absolved of the abduction of the Visitors' Seedlings! When news had gotten out via the solar system-wide professional media *and* the citizenry-based media, brief political rallies were held in major cities on Erth and Mars, and even on some of the independent space stations that were culturally aligned with Respect Hausa's philosophy.

There were, however, some legal backlash to the now-defunct Raid policy. Several Tellmondonian citizens on Asteropia felt it was bad enough that many of their ethnic brothers and sisters of Tell' heritage, were apprehended on Erth, Mars, and the myriad of space stations and habitats throughout Sol. But when a few Governance military-grade spaceships had actually *crossed* into the asteroid field—the entire belt *legally* claimed by the ancestors of the current Tell's, of a movement during the early 22nd century lead by a neo-Respect PunJon—that was at a political level of crossing Tellmondonian sovereignty! It would take a while, given the attention of the whole solar system on trying to placate the Visitors, but the Sol Governance had legally been sued by many of those Tellmondonian activists and many Tell' organizations that were generally antithetical to the Erth-based Governance to begin with...

After the small transporter had docked with *Gravity*, Respect Hausa emerged from the docking door; beaming as he walked his way to Mary Brushwell, whom was waiting for him in the main lobby of the ship. Indeed, *Gravity's* lobby was full of Tellmondonians and even some non-Tell's from Erth, Mars, and various stations! Like what had happened throughout the Sol system, they were all waiting for their specially arranged flight back to those very same locations in which the Governance had detained them...all being arranged by the Governance, of course. Prime Governor Valerio signed the special enactment for the arrangement.

Admiral Shan watched across the lobby as the elder Respect embraced the young student from the Martian University. Doctor Franks remained on Gravity, even after her help with the interrogation of Brushwell. It was by

Admiral Shan's request. The scientist was being extra-compensated by the Governance for her work with the admiral, and, again, truth be told, the educated Hausanite disciples were more likely to listen to *her* than to an admiral within the Governance machinery.

"Ok, boss," Dr. Franks quipped as she and the admiral looked on as the couple hugged in the midst of a cluster of Respect Hausa's followers, "what now?"

Admiral Shan thought for a bit as she watched *Gravity's* lobby being taken over by Hausa's tribalistic people. Many of Admiral Shan's officers and cadets were, *also*, looking on with some trepidation! She, then, glanced at her tall, thin friend from the Physical University and wondered within herself how they could have even been friends! For Dr. Franks *looked* as if she were one of the Protectors of the Seeds disciples that were just released from the Raid detention! But Reshma

Shan knew that she could never have a better friend than Dr. Franks, despite their cultural differences.

"Let's give them a few minutes," Shan said; a bit irritated. "And then have *both* of them meet me in my quarters...now's the time for *them* to play their part with the Visitors!"

Dr. Franks firmly nodded her head. "Agreed, Admiral."

As it turned out, it took about an hour before the elderly Respect and his young student primer to show up in Admiral Shan's private quarters. They were escorted by two Governance guards...there still was a trust factor with Respect Hausa. Indeed, the guards walked right into Admiral Shan's quarters, behind Respect Hausa and Mary Brushwell, at *their* surprise! Dr. Franks was seated at a posh chair not far from the admiral's large desk, where Shan was seated behind. The two guards took standing positions on opposite ends of Admiral Shan's quarters.

Respect Hausa lightly laughed as he and Mary took their respective seats. "I see you *still* don't trust me, my dear Admiral..."

Shan thought for a bit. "Ok, Respect Hausa, let's face it; *you* won! You were right about your fellow Respects and some of Asteropia's scientists experimenting on the Visitors' Seeds. Based on the communication technique I felt that one Seed did while at the spaceport on Pacificalis, I'm guessing all the Seeds that Asteropia's scientists experimented on had sent out some distress signal out to the Visitors!"

"You are correct about that, Admiral," he said from his chair. "It took a little while before the Visitors came for their young...frankly, a little longer than what Asteropian scientists had expected."

Admiral Shan and Dr. Franks looked at each other with surprised faces.

"So," Admiral Shan tried clarifying, "you *knew* that the Visitors would come for Humanity after the Asteropian scientists abducted their Seedling?" Shan then glanced at Mary. "Respect, I had the impression that you were *against* the taking of the Seeds from the Kuiper belt!"

"And that is still true! When I heard about it, as Mary told you, I'm sure, I tried to convince the Respects' Board *not* to go through with taking the Seeds, but my fellow Respects got greedy, dear Admiral...they were so anxious to be the first to obtain an alien life-force at the very edge of our solar system, they voted to let the Asteropian scientists to gather up some of the seeds!"

"On a planetoid," Dr. Franks ask earnestly.

The Respect was nodding. "That is correct, Dr. Franks. *But...*" He looked at Mary, whom had greeted him with a knowing smile. Respect Hausa returned his eyes to Admiral Shan and Dr. Franks. "Our blessed Visitors did not come *from* the Kuiper belt. They came from much farther out...they came from the Oort cloud!"

Admiral Shan and Dr. Franks looked at each other with surprised faces again, but this time their eyes were wide-opened! A thought occurred to the admiral.

"Now that I think of it, with the first abductions of *Governance* people, our Director Morelli Tuun's crew had said in the last of their recording that some objects were coming from the Oort section!"

The Respect nodded; his face, along with Mary, beaming. "Today, we call it *abducting* what the Asteropian scientists did with the Seeds several months ago. But it did not start off as an alien abduction—the aliens being humans, in this case!" He shrugged as he recalled the situation. "At first, none of us knew what those little, metal bits of technology were! Our scientists knew they were, obviously, alien—till this day, even Governance's records show that no known Sol-core societies had made it out as far as the Kuiper belt section since that one operation by that industrialist over 200 years ago—"

"Sigmund Cartwright," Dr. Franks threw in.

"That's it, Doctor...Cartwright, whom was also a Representative of what was *then* the governing Erth Industrial Alliance, had built an operation *only* on asteroid Quaoar. *Our* Asteropian scientists had discovered the Seeds on one of the smaller asteroids—at a *much* farther orbit than Quaoar! Actually, very *close* to the Oort cloud!"

"Highly unlikely that a private space entity of the 22nd century could make it *that* far out with the technology of their day," Mary interjected.

Both Admiral Shan and Dr. Franks nodded at her point. They let Respect Hausa continue.

"It was only *after* the scientists made it back to Asteropia from the Kuiper belt did we notice that the Seeds started to...communicate; vibrate;

sing...Asteropian scientists are *still* not sure what to call what the Seeds do when they communicate!"

"That's when you deduced that the Seedlings were sending out a distress signal," Admiral Shan guessed.

"Correct again, Admiral...those reinforced containers that Governance forces found them in during those Raids? Those cases weren't just to keep the Seeds dry!"

Then, Mary came in, "The cases are specifically built by Asteropian scientists to *block* the Seeds' signals...especially when some of the Tellmondonian scientists in Asteropia started experimenting with the Seeds!"

"And," the admiral speculated, the pieces beginning to click together for her, "somehow, one or a few of the Seeds got their signals out...which made it to the Visitors way out in the Oort cloud, and now we're in the mess we're in!"

Dr. Franks looked at Admiral Shan with a weary look. The admiral leaned back in her seat with a sigh before speaking. "Wish you had told me this at the spaceport on Pacificalis, Respect!"

"Would you have believed me? I'm sorry I lied about saying the Seed was a probe, Admiral Shan. But I was trying to use the Governance's power as a shield from my own brethren and sisters of Tellmondo! They discovered where I was at that time, and, well, I don't think you and the Governance body would've taken my side! With my eccentric personality known throughout Sol, and with some Tellmondonians in power who are not quite as open-minded as my followers and I about being one with all humans throughout the solar system, the Tell' Advisory Board would have simply built a story around me to convince the Governance that I was a fugitive of Asteropia, who'd stolen some alien beings!"

The admiral and the elder scientist shared a long look. Admiral Shan, then, dismissed the two guards that were standing in her quarters. She waited for them to leave and the door to her quarters shut before she got up from her desk and walked over to where the odd couple sat. Shan leaned back on her desk.

"Ok...you've convinced me, Respect. This meeting with Dr. Franks and I was actually meant as the last wall, to make sure we were on the same page, before I hand you your position for collecting those Seeds!"

Mary reached out and grasped Respect Hausa's hand. He simply smiled. The admiral went on.

"Now, this is *your* turn, Respect, to help us out in getting those Seedlings *back* to the Visitors! Mary did a good job in warning us that we only have so much time before the Visitors start making things uncomfortable for us... let's get you and Mary processed with a ship! I'll assign my people to work with you on recruiting from your disciples to help you."

Respect Hausa and Mary looked at one another. Mary pointed a thumb in the direction of the door to Admiral Shan's quarters. "Probably should catch all of his followers out in your lobby *before* they scatter throughout the solar system!"

CHAPTER 19

THREE WEEKS LATER. ABOARD THE SOL GOVERNANCE RECONNAISSANCE SHIP, #081; APPROACHING THE OUTER REGION OF THE KUIPER BELT...

"There's been another mass-abduction, Respect," Tellmondonian Hausa disciple AdamEve informed. He was at the ship's comm system, monitoring the news throughout the solar system.

The elder Respect winced for sadness and disappointment. He was at #081's command chair. "Where?"

"A grouping of space habitats near The Asteropia!"

"Is it me, or does it seem like the Visitors are abducting more Tell's lately," Olith, a middle-aged Hausanite, said from her station.

"Where the hell do the Visitors *keep* all our people," Lau'reign, in her thirties, asked as she walked over to another station in the ship's command suite. "What are we up to now? Over four-hundred thousand that the Visitors have snatched?"

"Now, now, my brothers and sisters," Respect Hausa lightly admonished from his command station. "Let's not forget to respect our Visitors from Sol's rim! Remember, *they* did not instigate this conflict."

Many of the Hausanite crew in the command suite glanced at one another. It was clear that some of Respect Hausa's followers were beginning to lose their adoration for the Visitors! After weeks of the Protectors of the Seeds quickly spreading out in large groups of teams throughout Sol to gather the remaining Seedlings that were still in the hands of other Hausanite disciples, they were finally near the Kuiper section of the solar system!

Scores of similar ships, issued by the Sol Governance, were following #081. Just as Mary Brushwell and Admiral Reshma Shan—whom was back on Pacificalis Island on Erth—had planned, the Hausanite followers from all over Sol had *voluntarily* handed over the Seeds they were protecting to Respect Hausa's Governance-created agency, "The Protectors' Return." The Protectors' fleet was on its last leg of returning those very Seeds that the Asteropian scientists had harvested from a very distant region in the Kuiper belt. But the Visitors' abduction of groups of humans throughout Sol were only getting larger in scope, and occurring more often!

"At least we're finally less than a day from the Kuiper belt," the Respect reminded his command crew, trying to encourage them.

'Yes, Respect,' came the uniform response from the whole command crew in the suite. The only two people that did *not* return the chant were Officers Daren Hopkins and Chase Tuuk. They were the *required* two Governance officers aboard #081, and each and every ship of The Protectors' Return fleet. *That* was one of the few prerequisites that Prime Governor Valerio had pushed, after the Governance Council voted to let Respect Hausa and his followers form their own mission.

Mary was commanding another Governance Reconnaissance ship, #271. Her team was in the midst of The Protectors' Return fleet...and it was from *that* ship that Respect Hausa had gotten an emergency contact from!

"Respect Hausa," the ship's Sentient said over a series of alarms as the interior lights switched to bright-red, "a series of the fleet's ships are in immediate danger of being targeted by the Visitors!"

Before the Respect even had time to respond, there was a direct comm from Mary. Respect Hausa answered as his command crew of Hausanite disciples were, now, working more like Governance officers!

"Hausa—!"

"I know, I know," he yelled back over the comm! "I'm switching to fleet-wide communique, Mary...Ok, Followers, remember we planned this out just in case, so let's be calm and implement what we practiced! We only have a few seconds, so we've got to make this count!"

Respect Hausa cut the open-comm and looked over at Lau'reign. "All the Seeds loaded?"

"Yes, Respect," she responded after a quick glance in her instruments.

Respect Hausa began another series of command until #081's Sentient interrupted.

"Respect...the Visitors' approach has halted!"

Everyone in the command suite froze! The communications of the other commanders of each Reconnaissance ship could be heard in the moment of silence.

By approximately two miles, what was one enormously bright ball of light had undergone a mitosis split by several other balls of light, though those subsequent structures were smaller than the prototype. Given it was space, there was no sound. However, like the tiny Seeds that were apprehended by humans throughout Sol, there were degrees of vibrations felt by everyone in every ship of The Protectors' Return fleet! Even some of the equipment aboard every ship had rattled or dropped to the floor, with the artificial gravity at work!

The spheres shimmered a tiny bit, and there was even some pulsing to them. The several spheres were spread out by miles between each one, and the largest ball was equidistantly in the center of that configuration. The Hausanite Protectors might as well had been near a small sun—but, without the heat!

There was a cry from everyone in #081! For no one had anticipated the Visitors' presence to be such an awe! Many in the ship whispered to themselves some form of prayer. Some were shocked into utter silence! All had to shield their eyes with their hands, due to the brilliance of the Visitors... and that was with each, respective Reconnaissance ships' sun-blocker!

"All ships, hold off on the ejection! Repeat, hold off on ejection," Respect Hausa finally said into the fleet-wide comm. "And make sure your ship's sun-protector is in working condition...it's no joke when I say we could all get some form of radiation sickness from the Visitors' very presence!"

"With respect, Sir," one of the scores of commanders, Darkened Energy, said over the comm, "but shouldn't we simply give them the Seeds *now*? That's what both sides are here for!"

"And what if they misinterpret our ejecting a multitude of Seeds as a *mass* of sorties," Respect Hausa shot back. His response, indeed, cooled down the explosion of voices over the fleet's comm.

"What are we doing, Respect Hausa," Mary put to him softly, but with enough urgency and formality to indicate to him it was time to make a decision!

Governance Officers Hopkins and Tuuk, from their respective stations, gave the Respect a questioning look... as per that required two Governance officers per Protectors' ship, the two Governance military troopers were to, physically, take over the command of the vessel should the situation get too hot for whomever was in command of the ship. Or, should Respect Hausa or any of his commanding disciples become incapacitated. But the Respect waved them off with one of his thin hands with a firm nod that he was ok.

He connected to the fleet-wide channel again. "Respect Hausa, here... like I said, we're going to hold off on launching the Seeds toward the

Visitors. I don't want them to mistake our actions as an assault! From what some of our scientists told me back on Asteropia, with their technological superiority to humans, the Visitors may, possibly, have the ability to obliterate Erth with *one bomb*!

"So, I'm not going to risk Humanity's existence on one rash move! I'm going to eject *one* of the Seedlings we have on #081...let them see our intentions, and what we have." The Respect cut the comm.

The Respect looked around the command suite, verifying one more time with the crew's reaction, that what he was planning was even plausible.

"Sentient..."

"Yes, Respect, I attentively listened to your statements...I am releasing one of the cases containing one, singular Seedling now."

It all seemed so anticlimactic. There was no *thud* or shaking of #081.

"Have we been recording our encounter, Sentient," Respect Hausa asked during the quiet time, just as the tiny case being ejected out into open space finally showed up on the ship's monitors. "Should something go wrong I want you to make sure this event's recording is sent to Sol-core...in case Humanity could glean something from this. I just hope our blessed Visitors are as—"

CHAPTER 20

SOL GOVERNANCE HEADQUARTERS; PACIFICALIS ISLAND...

"What," Admiral Shan exclaimed from her personal transporter. The image of Dr. Urla Franks was jerky and the audio was being drown out by other people's excited voices! "Urla, can you go to a quiet area where I can hear you?"

"They're back...they're back, Reshma...every damn one of them...!"

It was so loud where ever her good friend was, that Admiral Shan simply chose to close the call and got out of her personal vehicle that she had just parked as she arrived at one of the parking structures in the Governance headquarters facility. She jumped upon hearing loud bangs of fireworks further away, toward the downtown area of Pacificalis Island. Several more popping and splashing of colorful lights were seen seconds later. She frowned to herself...was today some holiday she had forgotten about?

Just then, her communicator had gone wild with calls! While the admiral was looking at her screen to see the identification of the several callers, another section of her communicator had a portion of the monitor devoted to news...and that's when she saw the unbelievable news of the returned humans from the Visitors!

Admiral Shan found herself screaming for joy! A small group of Governance officers, also in the parking structure, saw her and ran to Admiral Shan; thinking she was under attack! Then she explained to them the news. While she was uncontrollably telling the young group the news of the Visitors releasing *all* 4oo-thousand-plus humans that they had abducted, the young officers, also, started to get calls on their own communicators!

This went on for about thirty-minutes around the admiral. Various officers and cadets ran up to her and her constantly growing entourage! For they knew that *she* was the Governance's military official in charge of handling the Phenomenon with the Visitors!

By the time the large crowd around Admiral Shan made it to the main area of Headquarters, it was absolute mayhem! The news had long gotten to the Governance's home base before Shan had gotten back from, yet, another meeting across the Island!

Someone had requested to the base's Sentient to bring up one of the official news media's report on the Visitors...by the time a projected news cast was pulled up by the Sentient, a hush came over the large crowd in Headquarters' lobby.

The report showed a myriad of shaky images and vids of the Visitors taken by people throughout the several months of the Phenomenon. The media report also showed shots of every location where humans had been abducted by the Visitors: the Pluto area; the special class ship *The Justifier*; space station Watcher 2; the asteroid field of Asteropia; various space stations and habitats; Respect Hausa and his Hausanite disciples of the Protectors' Return fleet...

But then that same media had showed a sea of Humanity—it was every person that was abducted by the Visitors. As the media report played on, it was slowly becoming clear that something was strange about how and where they were shown in the report...how strange all the Returned faces were blank; as if they were some automatons, standing rod-straight.

And as the vid of the Returned panned out from that sea of Humanity, *where* they were, was becoming more clear: they were out in a field of tall grass. Somewhere in the United States, in its Great Plains region, perhaps...

And that report's image of the Returned kept panning out, until the pattern that was made with the standing, silent bodies was clear: the Returned were configured in such a way that they formed a stylized mock-up of the Sol system! To the left, a representation of Sol, and as one looked all the way to the right of that crude model of the solar system, it extended as far as Pluto. But, in that simple icon of the Sol system, made with the forever-silenced Returned, instead of a circle to represent Erth, there was a big, stylized 'X'!

A little warning from those who came for a visit from the edge of the solar system...

Printed in the United States
By Bookmasters